The Blooding of Jethro

The Blooding of Jethro

FRANK FIELDS

A Black Horse Western

ROBERT HALE · LONDON

© Frank Fields 1998
First published in Great Britain 1998

ISBN 0 7090 6231 1

Robert Hale Limited
Clerkenwell House
Clerkenwell Green
London EC1R 0HT

Photoset in North Wales by
Derek Doyle & Associates, Mold, Flintshire.
Printed and bound in Great Britain by
WBC Book Manufacturers Limited, Bridgend.

ONE

Frank Smith glanced up at the gathering dark clouds and announced that it looked like a bad storm brewing and that since it was late afternoon, they had better pull the wagon amongst a clump of trees for the night, especially since it was the only suitable spot they had seen all day and the small, clear stream was the only water they had encountered for more than two days, although if it was going to rain, water would probably not present a problem in the immediate future.

Frank and his family – wife Emma, daughter Mary, aged sixteen and son Jethro, aged nineteen – had left Philadelphia some four months earlier in the search for a new life and land in the West and were almost at the end of their long journey. According to Frank, another two weeks would see them reach their destination, although he had no real idea exactly where their destination was. All he had was a piece of paper issued by a government land office which apparently gave him title to some 200 acres of prime farming land. He wondered just what that piece of paper would really entitle him to, if anything at all, since it had only cost him five dollars.

Thus far their journey had been without any inci-
dents of note apart from being advised to make a
long detour round a desert which had added about a
week on to their time, and on one occasion, in the
middle of thick forest, having to sit and sweat as a
group of young Indians had inspected both them
and their wagon. The Indians had eventually left with
a couple of blankets, two knives and a bottle of
whiskey, all of which had been replaced a few days
later when they had passed through a small town.

The covered wagon was driven amongst the trees,
the mules unhitched and turned loose on the
comparatively lush grass and Emma Smith and her
daughter immediately set to preparing a meal. Jethro
announced that he would go and do some hunting
to try and supplement their sparse meal of dried
beans, salt beef, a little greyish flour – which seemed
more mites than actual flour – and some potatoes
which were really past cooking, but which were all
they had. Nobody objected, although they all
thought that Jethro was wasting his time since there
had been no sign of game for the past two days.
Jethro had in fact become quite adept at using his
rifle, his one prized possession, and he rarely missed
a chance to practise his skills. Jethro had been gone
about ten minutes when Frank Smith suddenly made
a grab for his rifle.

'We've got company,' he hissed, 'and I don't like
the look of them. Emma, Mary, hide behind the
wagon.' Both women obeyed the instruction just as
five dirty, unshaven riders appeared.

'Well now,' leered the man who appeared to be
the leader of the group, 'looks like we got us some

decent home cookin'. We ain't had no good home
cookin' in a long time. You won't mind if we join you
will you?' He did not wait for an answer but nodded
to the others and all dismounted, ignoring Frank
and his gun, seemingly more interested in Emma
and Mary. Frank raised his rifle slightly and threat-
eningly and immediately there was a coarse laugh
from the leader. 'He don't trust us!' he leered.
'That's right ain't it, feller, you don't trust us? You got
good judgement too; we ain't to be trusted, especially
when there's pretty women around.'

'They don't even have to be pretty,' grinned one of
the others, who appeared to have something wrong
with his foot as he limped quite pronouncedly.

'You make one move towards either of them and
I'll kill you,' threatened Frank, trying his best not to
appear too nervous. The leader once again laughed
coarsely and lunged at Mary. Frank's rifle was at his
shoulder, but he was too late. He fell to the ground
as a bullet thudded into his chest, fired by one of the
others.

'Frank!' screamed Emma, rushing to her husband's prostrate body. 'Frank! Answer me, Frank!'
There was no answer as she cradled his head in her
arms. 'What did you do that for?' she cried. 'We
haven't done anything to you.' She ripped aside his
shirt and looked at the wound and felt his heart, but
it was obvious that he was dead. She looked up and
screamed at the leader. 'Bastard! He's dead!'

'That was his own fault,' shrugged the man who
had fired the shot. 'He was goin' to shoot Pete. He
shouldn't've done that.'

'Yeh,' agreed Pete Watson, the leader of the
group. 'That warn't friendly at all; I was only goin' to

enjoy myself with that girl of yours. One thing you have to learn out here is that a man has to share things an' that includes his women.' Emma left the body of her husband and rushed to her daughter, clasping her close.

'Leave us alone!' she shouted. 'We didn't do anything to you, leave us alone, haven't you done enough damage?'

'Sure, we'll leave you,' grinned Pete. 'We'll leave you when we're good an' ready an' when you've served your purpose. Right now though, me an' my friends is hungry. You was preparin' a meal, get on with it, only this time make sure you cook enough for us all.'

Emma looked at her daughter who nodded weakly and both set about the task of preparing food even though both felt more like crying over the body of husband and father. However, if they had learned nothing else on their journey westward, it had been that few folk really cared what happened to anyone else and that violent death was to be expected at almost every turn. The fact that this was the first time they had encountered it themselves meant little, they had heard many stories of death and violence at the hands of renegade Indians and wandering outlaws. Emma had been tempted to tell these men that her son was out there somewhere, with a rifle, and that he was a very good shot, but Mary, sensing that this was what her mother was about to do, had whispered for her not to mention Jethro.

Jethro had found what, in his inexperienced mind, he thought were deer tracks and had followed them a lot further than he had intended before realizing that he was well away from where they had made camp. The deer tracks had finally disappeared completely and apart from one small lizard basking on a rock, he had seen no sign of life whatsoever. At first he was even uncertain as to which way the camp lay and when he heard a single shot in the distance, which helped to guide him, he did not place any particular significance to it, assuming that perhaps his father had seen something and was also hunting.

As he neared the camp, the threatened rain started, not gradually, but in a sudden, drenching downpour which seemed to become heavier as it continued. At first he sheltered in the lee of a large overhang, but when it did become obvious that there was going to be no immediate let-up in the rain, he carried on, finding it difficult for his smooth-soled boots to grip the now very muddy surface. Eventually he was within sight of the trees. A sudden scream above the beating rain made him freeze and it was then that he saw several horses. Apart from the scream, the sight of the horses told him that all was not right. Seemingly oblivious to the rain, he slowly made his way forward, trusted rifle at the ready – just in case.

The downpour had hit them suddenly, quickly putting out the fire over which Emma and Mary were cooking and they told the men that there was nothing they could do until the rain had stopped, which was not strictly true, they did have an old oil stove in the wagon, although they only had a very small amount of oil for it and did not normally use it unless they had to. This small setback did not appear to worry the men greatly and they all clambered into

the wagon, dragging both women behind them. One
of the men who had a pronounced humped back
and twisted, scarred face, leered at Mary, displaying
rotting, blackened teeth and then took a battered
deck of cards from his pocket and shuffled them.
Emma felt a sense of great relief as she thought that
they were going to pass the time by playing cards.

'Winner gets his choice!' grinned the humpback.
It was then that Emma realized just what they were
playing cards for. The cards were dealt out, five to
each man who then sorted them out into the best
possible hand. The winner turned out to be the
humpback who was immediately accused by the
others of cheating, but in a fairly lighthearted way. 'I
take her!' he leered, nodding at Mary. Emma choked
back a cry and held her daughter close. A second
hand was dealt out among the other four and this
time Pete won, but he had no choice, his prize would
be Emma.

The humpback pulled Mary away from the
embrace of her mother and dragged her forward. At
the same time Pete grabbed Emma, ripping at her
bodice with one hand and pulling up her skirts with
the other. The other three men laughed and jeered,
accusing their companions of not knowing what they
were doing and even if they did, of not being capable. Emma did not scream and did not resist too
hard, her experience as a mature, married woman,
making her realize the futility of such action, but
Mary had other ideas as she struggled against the
brute strength of the humpback. She screamed
loudly, which simply seemed to have the effect of
exciting the humpback even further. Eventually
brute strength won the day and when both men had

satisfied themselves, they were replaced by one of their companions. Eventually, after about half an hour, during which time both women were raped several times, Pete announced that he 'needed a shit' and clambered out of the wagon. His feet had hardly reached the ground when a bullet slammed into his shoulder. Pure instinct made him drop to the now muddy ground and roll beneath the wagon. In the meantime, the others, on hearing the shot, even above the sound of the rain and the noise they were making, had drawn their handguns and had lifted the edge of the canvas and were peering out in an effort to see whoever it was, but none of them was prepared to present themselves too openly.

Jethro needed no telling as to what was going on inside the wagon, the jeers and laughter and occasional scream painted a perfect picture, a picture confirmed when he noticed the body of his father. His first impulse had been to rush to the aid of his mother and sister, but common sense prevailed and, like it or not, all he could do was sit in the shelter of a tree and await developments.

The sight of a large figure clambering out of the wagon clutching his jeans to his waist proved too much for the inexperienced Jethro and before he really knew what he was doing, he had fired a shot, aiming for the man's chest – something which his father had always insisted was the correct thing to aim for. The fact that he had hit the man was obvious, but he did not know just where he had hit him or how badly he had injured him, although he did know that he had not killed the man. For a time everything went very quiet.

'Don't know who you are, mister!' called one of the men. 'But you shouldn't've done that. If it was one of the women you wanted, all you had to do was ask.'

'That's my ma an' my sister you've got in there!' responded Jethro.

'Ma an' sister!' laughed one of the men. 'Then take a look on the ground, that must be your pa, or should I say *was* your pa.'

'You'll never leave here alive!' threatened Jethro. 'I know how to use this gun.'

'I dare say you do,' called Pete from beneath the wagon, 'but there's five of us an' only one of you. It's you what's goin' to die, son, not us.'

'Jethro!' screamed his mother. 'Get away, get away while you can; there's no sense in you getting killed as well.'

'I can't just leave you!' called Jethro. 'They might kill you as well.'

'Leave us!' screamed his mother again. 'Look to yourself, we'll be all right.'

In the meantime, Pete had crawled from beneath the wagon, having pinpointed Jethro exactly and was at that moment circling round. The first Jethro knew about it was when a shot suddenly thudded into the tree trunk only a matter of an inch from his ear. He ducked and weaved his way through the trees knowing that he was being followed by at least two men, possibly all five. His biggest problem was not that he was frightened, the feeling had never even entered his head, but that he realized the only ammunition he had was that which was already loaded in his Winchester and he was uncertain as to just how many rounds it now held. Even if it had been fully loaded, he knew that against five guns he would not stand much chance. He ran, rain lashing in his face, not knowing where he was going, hoping to find somewhere to hide.

Suddenly he slithered to a stop and found himself looking down an almost sheer drop of perhaps thirty or forty feet with no obvious way down. He turned and waited for his pursuers to approach. . . .

Pete Watson, clutching at his bleeding shoulder, nodded to Humpback Chisholm who was a few yards behind him and indicated Jethro who was standing in the open, his rifle at the ready but plainly not having seen either of them.

'He's yours!' whispered Pete. 'Young bastard put a bullet through my shoulder.'

Humpback's twisted mouth leered at the thought as if nothing pleased him better than killing other men and he raised his handgun, took a steady aim, clasping the gun with both hands, his feet spread slightly apart, and fired.

Jethro twisted round as the bullet struck home, slithered on the wet mud and suddenly disappeared over the sheer drop. Both men rushed forward and peered down to see Jethro's apparently lifeless body lying partly in a pool of muddy water. They looked about for a way down so that they could make certain that he was dead, but could not find a way, especially one they could negotiate in the driving rain, Pete eventually indicated to Humpback that they should get back to the wagon and the women.

'That's both your men dead,' Pete announced, as both Emma and Mary peered anxiously from the wagon. 'That just leaves you two. Now, we is hungry,

I saw an oil stove in the wagon, use it; we want some hot food an' we want it quick.'

Emma and Mary managed to choke back their tears, knowing full well that neither grief nor tears were part of the vocabulary or feelings of these men and at that moment all they could hope for was that they would eventually be allowed to live, after they had served their purpose in satisfying the men's lust. Emma was forced to clean and bandage Pete's wound and she told him it appeared that the bullet had passed straight through and the wound was perfectly clean. Eventually a meal of salt beef, potatoes, beans and pancakes was served to the men, who appeared to appreciate even what was very basic cooking.

Once the meal was finished, all five searched through the wagon for anything of use or value, especially money. Humpback gave whoops of joy as he uncovered two bottles of whiskey and immediately took a large swallow, choking and spluttering as the coarse liquid seared his throat. Nevertheless, he declared it to be 'good stuff' and took another pull at the bottle. The unopened bottle was snatched from his grasp by one of the others and soon all five were taking long drinks and gradually becoming the worse for it. Although now quite drunk, their search continued and Pete did find some money, about twenty dollars, which he quickly stuffed into his pocket. Various items of men's clothing were commandeered and stuffed into saddle-bags and Humpback dressed himself in one of Emma's dresses and paraded round to the laughs and jeers of the others. Eventually though, their attention turned back to the women.

*

Emma's hand reached out to comfort her daughter, who was lying naked but held down by the arm of one of the men. It had been dark for quite some time, neither of them having any idea what time it was except that it must have been at least midnight. Emma had managed to free herself from the obscene embrace of Humpback and, at her mother's touch, Mary, too, tried to free herself, but at first the dirty, hairy arm simply tightened.

'I have to go!' whispered Mary into the ear of the man.

'Go where?' mumbled the man, more asleep than awake.

'I need to . . . you know, I need to go!' whispered Mary.

'If you want a piss or a shit, just say so,' mumbled the man.

'Yes, that's it,' Mary whispered again, trying to force the arm off her. 'I must go. Please let me go.'

'Piss where you are,' grumbled the man. 'It won't hurt nobody.'

'What about . . .' croaked Mary. 'I need to do the other.'

'Christ!' he oathed. 'OK, OK, but don't take too long.'

Mary crawled over him, followed by her mother, who managed to grab a couple of blankets and each covered themselves against the cool, night air. Emma placed a comforting arm around her daughter and for a few moments neither woman could control their emotions as they cried into each other's arms. Suddenly Emma choked back her tears as she saw the

body of her husband highlighted in a shaft of moonlight streaming through a break in the clouds. Mary,
too, turned to look at her father and, as they stared
in sorrowful silence, the moonlight also highlighted
Frank's rifle, which none of the outlaws had bothered to pick up. It appeared that the same idea came
to both Emma and her daughter simultaneously.

Looking about and listening to the snores of the
outlaws for a time before either of them dared to
move towards the gun, Mary eventually decided that
one of them had to make the move and quickly went
forward, picked up the rifle and hid it under her
blanket. It appeared that she had done so just in
time, as suddenly two of the men tumbled out of the
wagon, demanding to know what was taking the
women so long. Mary stared at them and then down
at the body of her father, hoping that they would not
realize the rifle was missing.

'I was just payin' my respects to my pa,' she said.
'You might allow us that much at least.'

'It ain't goin' to do him much good,' snarled
Humpback, snatching at her arm and almost making
her drop the rifle. 'C'mon, it's my turn with you.'
The other man grabbed at Emma and forced her
into the wagon.

Mary somehow managed to slip the rifle under a
pile of clothing close to where Humpback forced her
down, not really knowing if she would ever be in a
position to use it – which she was quite determined
to do if at all possible – or even if she really could,
despite her determination. Jethro had taught her
how to hold a rifle, but she had never actually fired
one. However, the thought of revenge for the death
of her father and brother and the treatment both she

and her mother had received at the hands of the five
men, convinced her that she would have no difficulty
in killing all of them. The remainder of the night
passed slowly as their torment continued into the
early hours.

Nobody seemed particularly interested in breakfast
and all five men awoke in foul tempers. Interest in
the women seemed to have vanished – a situation
Emma was keen to encourage as she and Mary kept
well away from any of them.

Mary managed to position herself close to the
wagon and within reach of the rifle and was biding
her time. At first, it seemed as if neither she nor her
mother existed as far as the men were concerned
but, just as Pete had ordered the others to saddle
their horses, he and Humpback suddenly turned on
Emma, Humpback laughing as he pointed his handgun at her head.

'Thought we'd forgotten about you, didn't you?'
he leered. 'I was just thinkin' that a married woman's
place is by her husband's side an' since your old man
is dead, that means you should be dead too. I hear
tell of some place abroad where a woman has to
climb aboard her husband's coffin while they burn it.
I guess that means she gets burned too. I ain't
expectin' you to burn, but the best place for you is at
your old man's side.'

In the meantime, Mary had slipped her hand into
the wagon and found the rifle and at the sight of her
mother about to be shot, she raised the gun as she
had been taught, closed her eyes and squeezed the
trigger. . . .

She heard the shot close to her ear, she felt the

jerk of the rifle and she heard a cry of pain. The only trouble was that the cry of pain she heard was her own. It was the last thing she ever heard.

Pete Watson looked down at Mary's crumpled, blood-ied body and shook his head as he holstered his gun. Humpback Chisholm pulled a gold ring off the finger of Emma Smith and then wiped his dirty hand across her lifeless body.

'You all right?' Pete asked Humpback.

'Just a scratch,' muttered Humpback, showing a graze on his upper arm where the bullet from Mary's rifle had singed him. 'What about the other feller?' he said. 'Somebody ought to make sure he's dead.'

Pete dispatched one of the others to check and after about five minutes he returned and announced that he was dead, at least he was lying in a pool of water and looked dead. This appeared to satisfy both Pete and Humpback and all five eventually left the scene of carnage.

TWO

Jethro felt very cold and wet. It took him quite some time to focus his eyes and even when he did there was nothing much to see except a grey, cloudy sky. He tried moving his arms and legs but they stubbornly refused to obey, almost as if they had become frozen solid by continued exposure to the cold and wet. After a time, he managed to turn his body slightly, giving him a view of the cliff, now streaming with water. About ten minutes later his arms started to function and he was able to force himself into an upright position and it was then he realized that he was sitting in a pool of muddy water. Removing himself from the pool proved rather more difficult than it looked as his legs buckled beneath him, not helped by the slimy mud and a sharp pain in his left shoulder which made using that arm to lever himself up almost impossible. His other hand went up to where the pain was but he could not feel anything and it was only when he looked at the palm of his hand that he realized that blood was mixed with the wet on his shirt. He tried lifting his arm, but the effort proved too painful. Then he looked up at the sky and grunted when he saw that it was daylight, although he was uncertain if he had been lying at the foot of the cliff for only a few minutes, a few hours or even a few days. Eventually he decided that he had been there since the previous evening. Slowly, memories of that previous night came back to him and it was the thought of what might have happened to his mother and sister which spurred him on and overcame his pain and discomfort.

He found his rifle on the edge of the pool, now covered in mud and showing signs of rust in a couple of places. After wiping most of the mud off, he looked for a way up the cliff. It took him about twenty minutes to find a way up and reach the top and another ten minutes to trek back to the trees and the wagon. The sight which greeted him filled him with despair, although he shed no tears. In his heart he had known what to expect.

The two mules were still munching contentedly on the grass among the trees and, apart from the fact that the wagon had obviously been searched, it was otherwise intact, which surprised him; he had expected to find it either burned out or completely wrecked. He gathered the bodies of his parents and sister together and stood silently over them for a few minutes, offering up a silent prayer and then had to decide whether or not to bury them or take their bodies on to the next town. He did not like the thought of burying them in the middle of nowhere without the dignity of a Christian burial, if only for his mother's sake; she had been a very religious person, some of which had rubbed off on him. The only trouble was that he had no idea just how far away the next town was and even he knew that he could not carry the bodies around too long, the heat of the day soon made flesh decay. In the end, he decided to take the bodies and allow himself two days to reach a town and if by that time he had not found anywhere, he would bury them wherever he happened to be. Lifting the bodies into the wagon proved very difficult, especially that of his father who was a big man, but eventually, after a lot of heaving, struggling and even swearing, they were aboard and covered with blankets.

Before he set out, he cleaned and oiled his rifle, found a box of bullets which had been missed in the search, loaded the gun and then fired a single shot just to make certain that it was still working properly, which it appeared to be. He also checked the secret compartment underneath the wagon – something his father had insisted on having – which contained the land certificate and all the money they had apart from a few dollars kept within reach in the wagon. The money in the wagon had been found but, luckily, the $500 and the land certificate in the secret compartment were untouched.

Harnessing and hitching the mules to the wagon was something of a trial, his shoulder was now even more painful than before, which he put down to strain but felt very much as though the bullet was still lodged in it, After almost an hour, he had the mules in harness and hitched and had started on his way West.

By mid-afternoon the trail had dried out and the going was much easier as it became quite flat. His biggest problems were the numerous small gullies and rivers which were now full of water and quite difficult to negotiate.

*

That first night was spent alongside a muddy water-hole and, while the mules did not seem to mind, he would not risk drinking the water. Fortunately the water barrel attached to the side of the wagon was still about a quarter full. He had not even considered refilling it from the stream where they had camped or from any of the many streams and rivers he had encountered. Now all there was was one dirty water-hole. His meal that evening consisted of chewing on a piece of salt beef, which had the effect of making him feel quite ill during the night.

The second night found him pulling alongside a fairly wide river where the trail divided, one fork going through the river at what was plainly a ford when the water level was lower, although at that moment a crossing would have been impossible, and the other fork following the river. The decision as to which way to go was made for him since crossing was out of the question, plus the fact that he found a battered sign which indicated that some place called Henderson was another thirty miles along the trail which followed the river and that somewhere named Hart was forty miles through the ford. Apart from having little choice of where to go, he reasoned that Henderson was in a westerly direction and the road to Hart would take him in a more northerly direction and since West was the direction they had been heading, that was the way he had to go. However, he felt very tired and very sore and decided to stay where he was for the night. Having sampled the uncooked salt beef the previous night, he decided that it was one luxury he could well afford to miss. It was obvious that there was game about, he had seen at least three rabbits and two large, plump birds, but the pain in his shoulder stopped him from trying to catch any. With luck he would reach Henderson in two days at the most.

Henderson was an average-sized town consisting of one main street and three or four smaller side streets. The main industry appeared to be centred on timber if the large timber mill on the edge of town was anything to go by. As he approached the town he passed several farms and, for a time, followed a rail-road which ended at the timber mill. The rust on the tracks indicated that trains did not come too often, probably only when there was sufficient timber. His arrival attracted little attention other than some folk seemed surprised that he appeared to be alone. He later learned that settlers' wagons were a common sight through the town. His first call was to the sher-iff's office which was conveniently next door to a shabby-looking eating house, but at that moment he was hungry enough to try anything. Sheriff Wally Hutchinson listened to the young man's story as both sat at the only table in the eating-house and, slowly and sympathetically, shook his head as Jethro hungrily set into a mess of minced meat, beans, turnip greens and potatoes.

'Could you identify these men?' he asked.

'I only caught sight of the one I shot at,' said Jethro. 'I seem to remember hearing some names though.' He had been thinking about that ever since starting out and was quite certain of the names he had heard. 'One was called Pete; Pete *what* I don't know. One was called Clubfoot, at least that's what it

sounded like. . . .' The sheriff showed sudden interest at the mention of that name. 'And I'm quite
certain that the name Curly was mentioned.'

'Any others?' urged the sheriff. 'What about Ernie
or Humpback?'

'No, I didn't hear any others,' said Jethro. 'Is it
important?'

'Not really,' sighed the sheriff. 'I think five of the
most notorious men in the West paid you a visit.
You're damned lucky to be alive; other settlers'
wagons have been found in the past with everyone
slaughtered. There's been nothing we could ever pin
on them – Pete Watson, Ernie Price, Clubfoot
Higgins – he has a deformed foot, that's why they call
him Clubfoot – Curly Johnson – he's completely bald
– and Humpback Chisholm. He's the meanest and
ugliest of them all; you'd recognize him anywhere
even if you had never seen him before. He has a big
hump on his back, slightly to one side which makes
his shoulders look odd, a twisted, scarred face which
looks like he was slammed against somethin' as a
baby. He's likely to kill a man just because he don't
like the colour of his shirt.'

'If they're so well known, why haven't they been
arrested?' asked Jethro.

'It's easy to see that you're fresh out from the
East,' smiled the sheriff. 'Sure, everyone knows who
they are an' what they do, but so far nobody has been
able to get enough evidence together to charge 'em,
at least none that'd stand up in court and the few
who might've been able to testify have either refused
for various reasons or even suddenly disappeared.'

'Try me,' offered Jethro.

'Son,' smiled Wally, 'I appreciate what you're

sayin', but you didn't actually see any of them properly and any half-baked lawyer could shoot down your story about hearin' the names. Now, you look to be in a bad way, you'd better get along to see Doc Galloway as soon as you've eaten that.'

'First I have to see about gettin' my folks a proper burial,' said Jethro. 'I've got some money, I can pay for proper coffins and plots in the churchyard.'

'You get yourself down to Doc Galloway,' insisted the sheriff. 'I'll go see the minister an' the undertaker.' Jethro thought about it and then nodded. 'The doc's office is halfway down the street opposite; the big house on its own, there's a sign outside. Tell him I sent you.'

Jethro grimaced slightly and moved his shoulder. 'It does seem to be getting worse,' he nodded. 'OK, thanks Sheriff, but don't let anyone go buryin' my folks before I can be there.'

'I'll tell 'em,' nodded Wally. 'By the way, do you intend sleepin' in that wagon tonight?'

'I haven't got anywhere else to go,' said Jethro. 'Is there a problem?'

'You'd better pull it behind the timber mill,' said Wally. 'Folk don't take too kindly to havin' covered wagons spread all over the town. Oh, an' don't leave anythin' of any value in it when you're not there, some of our younger citizens have very sticky fingers.'

'I'll do that,' said Jethro. He finished his meal and crossed the street.

Doc Galloway's house and office was a very imposing-looking building and the whole of the front ground floor seemed to be given over to what was virtually a small hospital. There were two other patients waiting to see the doc and despite the obvious seriousness of his injury, Jethro was ordered to wait his turn by a middle-aged woman. Fifteen minutes later, Doc Galloway, a tubby, middle-aged, bespectacled man, was tutting quietly as he examined the wound.

'The bullet's still in there,' he declared. 'It's got to come out. Leave it much longer and gangrene will set in. As it is I'm going to have to take some rotten flesh away.'

'It can't be that bad!' exclaimed Jethro, quite alarmed at the prospect. 'It only happened four or five days ago.'

'Long enough to get infected,' said the doc. 'Out here I've known gangrene to set in in less than a day. The choice is yours, young feller. I operate now or you join your folks in a few days.'

'How long will it take?' asked Jethro. 'I have to see to the funeral arrangements and I want to be there when they're buried.'

'You won't be in no fit state to go anywhere for a couple of days,' said the doc. He sighed and studied the young man's face for a while. 'OK, I'll tell you what: you go and have your funeral today. The minister won't mind and I'm sure Sam Trickett, the undertaker, will soon have some coffins knocked together, if he hasn't already got some. You have your funeral, pay your respects to your kin and then come back here. The operation itself won't take long, maybe twenty minutes, but it'll take you a whole lot longer to recover from your hangover.'

'Hangover?' queried Jethro.

'Yes,' grinned the doc, 'hangover! On the way back, call in the saloon for a bottle of whiskey, the cheapest will do and the effect is quicker.'

'What do I want whiskey for?' Jethro asked.

'To knock you out,' the doc grinned again. 'Before I cut into you, you should be past caring after a bottle of rough whiskey.'

'Don't you have anything else?' said Jethro, now very alarmed. 'Back East I hear they've got some kind of gas which knocks you out.'

Doc Galloway laughed. 'Yes, I hear things like that too. There's just one slight problem, this isn't the East and we don't have the sophisticated equipment those fancy Eastern doctors have. Maybe one day things like that might reach out this far, but for the moment the best thing we have for knocking you out is whiskey.'

Jethro realized that he had very little choice in the matter and, although he did not really relish the thought of making himself drunk on whiskey, he knew that it was probably the easiest way. Promising to return to the doc's office as soon as the funeral had taken place, he went to the sheriff's office where he found a crowd of people staring into his wagon. They moved aside self-consciously as Jethro approached.

'Sam Trickett has taken the bodies,' said Wally Hutchinson, as Jethro entered the office. 'What did Doc Galloway have to say?'

'He's got to cut into me,' grimaced Jethro. 'He told me to buy a bottle of whiskey. What about the minister, can he bury them now?'

'All in hand, son,' smiled Wally. 'I guessed the doc would have to operate on you an' I guessed he'd give you time to bury your folks. When you buy the whiskey, you tell Jimmy behind the bar what you want it for, he has a special brew guaranteed to lay you out flat. Everybody uses it when the doc's got some cuttin' to do. I wouldn't worry about Doc Galloway, he's the best there is.' Jethro did not doubt the ability of the doc, only his method.

At that moment a clergyman came into the office, saw Jethro and proffered his hand as he smiled thinly. 'Ah, you must be the young man whose parents and sister I am to bury. Pleased to meet you, young man, and please accept my deepest condolences. To lose one member of one's family by natural means is bad enough but to lose three by the actions of others must be . . . well, you must understand what I am trying to say.' Jethro simply nodded. 'At least you brought them for a proper Christian burial instead of leaving them to be eaten by the buzzards and coyotes.' Jethro had not thought about buzzards and coyotes when he had decided not to bury them himself, but he recalled stories about coyotes being able to dig up bodies more than six feet under the ground.

'How much do I owe you?' he asked.

'My dear boy,' grinned the minister. 'I make no charge for such a service. There is a charge of two dollars for each grave, for the men who have to dig them, you understand. I make no charge for my services, but you are quite free to make a donation if you so wish. The coffins, of course, have to be paid for, but you must deal with Mr Trickett on that.' Jethro nodded his agreement and the minister, the Reverend James Gough, continued, 'I have just come from Mr Trickett and he tells me that he has two coffins ready which are just the right size for your mother and sister and that he is even now making a

larger one to take your father. He says it will be about
another fifteen minutes. If you wish, you may see the
bodies before he nails down the lids, he has a small
chapel of rest at the side of his yard.'

'Yes,' said Jethro, choking slightly, 'I'd like to see
them one last time.'

'I'll escort you,' offered the minister. 'You may
take as long as you wish; I expect my grave-diggers
will require a little more time as it is not often they
have to dig three graves at once and they usually get
at least two days' notice. I think under the circumstances, providing you can afford it, of course, it
might be a nice gesture to offer them twice their
usual fee.'

'I'll see to it,' nodded Jethro. 'Now, I'd like to be
with my family for a while if you don't mind.' The
Reverend James Gough smiled and led the way out of
the office and along the street to a building marked
'Samuel Trickett – Undertaker and Joiner – Quality
Furniture Made to Order'.

He was shown into a small but tastefully furnished
room rather like a small church where two coffins
were already laid on trestles, the coffins containing
the ashen-faced bodies of his mother and sister. He
stood silently between the two for some time, his
hands resting one on each of their shoulders. A short
time later two men struggled in with the third coffin
which they placed on two more trestles. With three
coffins in the tiny room there was hardly space left.
Jethro moved to stand near his father and once again
rested a hand on his shoulder.

'I'll get them, Pa,' he whispered hoarsely. 'You
hear that, Ma, Mary? I'll track them down and kill
them even if it takes me the rest of my life. I promise

I won't rest until all five are dead. I know who they are so finding them shouldn't be too hard. It might be a bit of time before I can start out though, I took a bullet in the shoulder, but from where you're lookin' you probably know that. Anyhow, Doc Galloway has to operate on me, but that should be all right. The other thing I have to do is get me a hand-gun, you know, one of those revolvers and learn how to use it. I can't rely on using a rifle all the time. I know you never approved of those kind of guns, Pa, but this time I think you will.'

He stood in silence for a time, praying quietly when he became aware of someone standing by the door. He turned to see the Reverend Gough and another man, dressed in black suit and top hat with a dark ribbon round it. He guessed this was Samuel Trickett – Undertaker and Joiner – Quality Furniture Made to Order.

'If you are quite ready, Mr Smith,' smiled the minister. 'Mr Trickett would like to have the coffins nailed down and carried to the hearse and I have had word that the graves are ready.'

Jethro looked down at his father, patted his shoulder and turned to his mother and sister and gently kissed each of them on the cheek. Wiping away a tear he nodded to the undertaker and went out into the street. He was rather surprised to see a large, glass-sided hearse and was even more surprised when all three coffins were fitted in to it. He had not really known what to expect, but his travels had conditioned him into expecting less and less the further West they were. He would not have been surprised at the hearse being nothing more than a wagon.

Inevitably, a curious crowd had gathered, most just

to stare, but two elderly ladies, appropriately dressed in black, seemed to be prepared to follow the funeral procession, a procession which he had expected to consist only of himself and the Reverend James Gough. In the event, the procession was made up of himself and the minister immediately behind the hearse, the two elderly ladies behind them and six other people – four women and two men – behind the two ladies.

'The Misses Macdiarmid,' explained the Reverend Gough. 'I don't think they've missed a funeral for the past fifty years. I know I can always rely on the Misses Macdiarmid for funerals, weddings, christenings and all my dreary services.'

'What about the others?' whispered Jethro. 'I don't know any of them.'

'The two men always attend funerals when they can,' explained the minister. 'I do believe they get some strange form of enjoyment from it. They certainly are not too regular in their attendance at church. The ladies, too, seem to enjoy funerals, but I rarely see them at christenings or weddings. At least your parents will have a better send off than they might have expected.'

The distance from the funeral parlour to the church was no more than 300 yards, but it took them quite a long time and once again Jethro was surprised at just how many people, men in particular, doffed their hats and stood with heads bowed as the procession went by.

The service itself was mercifully short, taken at the graveside and when the minister had said his piece, the two grave-diggers lost no time in filling in the graves. Without his having asked for them, Samuel

Trickett produced three wooden crosses, each bearing the names of his mother, father and sister, handing them to Jethro to press into the ground. Everyone except Jethro and the Misses Macdiarmid withdrew. For a time Jethro stood, head bowed at the foot of the graves. Only when he decided to leave did the Misses Macdiarmid also leave, smiling at Jethro as he allowed them through the cemetery gate ahead of him but not saying a thing. He joined the Reverend James Gough inside the church and handed him twenty-five dollars.

'May I leave you to pay the grave-diggers, Reverend?' he said. 'The rest is for you, I hope it's enough.'

'My dear boy!' beamed the minister. 'Most generous of you, most generous indeed. I have no doubt that Mr Trickett will present you with his account.' He pushed the three notes into his pocket beneath his cassock and patted his hip. 'Most generous of you, yes indeed. It has given me inspiration for my sermon on Sunday.'

'You know,' smiled Jethro. 'I don't even know what day of the week it is. When you're travelling it's too easy to lose all track of time.'

'Today is Friday,' said the minister. 'I understand you are to be operated on by Doctor Galloway. I wish you luck, my son.'

'Luck?' queried Jethro, looking sharply at the minister. 'Shall I need luck?'

'No, no, of course not,' laughed the minister nervously. 'Doctor Galloway is the best there is. It was just a figure of speech.' It might have been a figure of speech but it did little to allay Jethro's anxiety.

Samuel Trickett was waiting for Jethro as he left

the church and he too wished him luck with regards the attentions of Doc Galloway and would it be inconvenient if Mr Smith could pay for the coffins and the hearse before he saw the doctor? This comment, too, did little to calm his growing concern, but Jethro was forced to smile and handed over the fifteen dollars asked for. He had the distinct feeling that he had been overcharged by both the undertaker and the minister, although he had given the minister his money voluntarily, but he noted that it had not been refused as being too much. After checking with Sheriff Wally Hutchinson, who had had the wagon removed to a patch of ground behind the timber mill, Jethro went to the saloon where he saw Jimmy, the bartender, told him what he wanted the whiskey for, was again wished the best of luck and assured that there was nobody better than Doc Galloway – something he was certainly having grave doubts about since everyone wished him the best of luck – and was charged two dollars for an unlabelled bottle of whiskey and advised to start drinking it straightaway. He decided to take this advice and, by the time he presented himself to Doc Galloway, he had managed to drink about a third of the contents. However, the doc insisted that he kept on drinking either until he had drunk the entire bottle or until he passed out. He never did find out which came first.

THREE

Jethro woke up to a blinding headache and flashes before his eyes and it took a few minutes for the flashes to settle down and a while longer for him to realize that he was lying in the covered wagon, although he could not remember either being carried there or making his own way. In fact, his memories of the previous day were very hazy. He doubted very much if he had made his own way to the wagon since even then he was obviously incapable of walking. Whether this was due to the operation on his shoulder or the whiskey seemed a moot point, but he tended to come down in favour of the effects of the whiskey. He had only ever been drunk once before in his life and that at the age of twelve when he had found a bottle of his father's whiskey and had drunk most of it and regretted it ever since and had always vowed never to touch the stuff again.

He tried moving his left arm and found the effort quite painful and lifted his other hand to his shoulder only to discover that he was swathed in bandages. A faint glimmer of light through the closed covers of the wagon seemed to indicate that it was daylight and he even wondered which day it was.

The cover was suddenly thrown back and two blurred faces appeared, one of which he vaguely recognized as belonging to Sheriff Wally Hutchinson and the other eventually came into focus as being that of Doc Galloway. Both men climbed into the wagon and said something which Jethro could not understand, but the doc immediately unfastened the bandages and seemed to be talking to himself as he examined the wound.

'Looks fine to me,' said the doc, after a few grunts and nods, this time his voice more distinct. 'Another week should see it OK. You're a lucky feller,' he continued. 'I reckon another day and there would have been nothing I could have done for you, the gangrene was worse than I thought and when it gets into somewhere like a shoulder or chest it isn't like a leg or arm which can be chopped off, you just die, slowly and in agony. Are you right-handed or left-handed?'

Jethro had to think about that one, his muddled state of mind seemed incapable of immediately working it out. 'Right!' he said eventually, after mentally moving each hand. 'At least I think so. Yes, definitely right-handed,' he added.

'Good,' said the doc. 'Your left side is probably going to be a lot weaker from now on, but if you're right-handed it won't matter all that much.' He cleaned up the wound again and redressed it. 'You come and see me in two days,' he instructed. 'We don't want it turning bad again.' He clambered out of the wagon leaving Jethro alone with the sheriff.

'I took charge of your money,' said Wally. 'It don't pay to have that much cash on you, especially in the condition you were in. It's in my safe in the office; you can have it back whenever you want. I took the liberty of payin' the doc his twenty dollars, I hope that's OK'

'Sure,' nodded Jethro. 'Thanks. I presume I've been unconscious all night, what time is it now?'

'Nine in the mornin',' replied the sheriff. 'You've been out somethin' like sixteen hours.'

'It could be sixteen days as far as I'm concerned,' said Jethro, grinning weakly. 'I shouldn't drink so much. I don't think I ever want to see a bottle of whiskey again.'

'Jimmy's special is wicked stuff,' laughed Wally. 'Think you can get up?'

'I reckon so,' said Jethro, managing, with a little help from Wally, to get into a sitting position. For a couple of minutes his head rebelled against this new position but it eventually conceded defeat and the world stopped revolving quite as fast and things slowly began to get back to something like normal. Despite the effects of the whiskey and the cutting Doc Galloway had inflicted on him, Jethro suddenly felt very hungry. 'I need somethin' to eat,' he mumbled. 'Is that eatin'-house still open?'

'Never closes,' laughed Wally. 'Come on. I'll give you a hand to get out.' He helped Jethro out of the wagon and accompanied him back to his office and the eating-house next door. Jethro suggested that it might not be a bad thing if Wally was to keep the money in his safe until he was well enough to decide what he was going to do next, but he did take two five-dollar bills out of it for immediate expenses.

It appeared that there were only two choices ever available at the eating-house, run by a very fat and rather dirty-looking woman who said that her name was Grace Stallard and that she was willing, for a fee, to provide other more personal services should Jethro require them. The other personal services did not appeal to him nor did the choice of minced beef or beef stew, but the menu was more appealing than any delights Grace Stallard may have had to offer. He ate his meal of beef stew and stodgy dumplings with turnip greens and washed the whole down with a large mug of coffee, which tasted surprisingly good and he promised to consider Grace's other offer. Apart from her size, she was plainly almost twice his age, both of which turned him off. Besides, although nineteen years of age, the nearest he had been to any woman on anything like intimate terms, had been seeing his mother and sister in various states of undress on their journey.

Despite the indifference of the meal, he certainly felt much better for it and wandered down to the church and cemetery where he stood in silence at the foot of the graves of his parents and sister for quite some time, his mind a jumble of grief, anger and promises to avenge them. He must have been standing there about ten or fifteen minutes when he became aware of someone standing nearby, watching him. He turned to see the Reverend James Gough.

'I did not want to interrupt your thoughts,' smiled the reverend. 'I hear that the operation went well, I'm pleased for you.'

'I was going to ask about that,' said Jethro, turning away from the graves and walking towards the minister. 'Why did everyone wish me the best of luck all the time? It was almost as if they had little faith in Doc Galloway.'

The Reverend Gough smiled and nodded. 'Unfortunately, although he is an excellent doctor and very good surgeon,' he said, 'Doc Galloway is well known for a tendency to be just as drunk as his patients when he performs an operation. There have been one or two shall we say, unfortunate, accidents with his scapel. I gather that you were lucky and that he did not take courage from the bottle before he cut into you.' Jethro smiled and nodded, his hand automatically feeling his injury.

'I know maybe I shouldn't be asking a man like you this kind of question,' said Jethro, 'but what do you know about some men named, Pete Watson, Ernie Price, Clubfoot Higgins, Curly Johnson and Humpback Chisholm? Everyone seems to know who they are.'

The reverend nodded sagely. 'I understand the reason for your question,' he said. 'I have heard that you believe it was these men who killed your family and I can appreciate what your thoughts must be at this moment, but, as a minister, I must ask you to consider seriously what you feel you must do.'

'And what do you think I feel?' asked Jethro.

'Vengeance!' smiled the minister. 'Right now you are intent on seeking out these men and exacting retribution. I could see it in your face as you stood over the graves. It is a natural reaction. Remember, "Vengeance is mine, said the Lord".'

'Well it seems to me that both the Lord and the law are powerless,' said Jethro. 'The sheriff needs proof and that's the one thing which is lacking. I think I am a good Christian, Reverend, but please don't ask me not to at least consider taking vengeance. If I don't do something, who can? Does everyone have to wait until some other unfortunate travellers or even local farmers have been killed before anything is done?'

'I do not condemn you for what you feel,' sighed the minister. 'Vengeance is an all too natural feeling in any man, even within myself on occasion. Yes, I, too, have been tempted in that direction in more than one instance. All I ask is that you think seriously about it.'

'I think I've done my share of thinking,' said Jethro. 'OK, Reverend, I'll do what you ask and give it some more thought, but don't expect miracles.'

'This is not the land where miracles happen,' smiled the minister.

Jethro left the Reverend James Gough and wandered back into the main street where he came across a general hardware store which sold guns, one in particular in the window catching his eye, a long-barrelled Colt.

'Best handgun in the world,' enthused the store owner, Hans Gruber, a man of German origin who still talked with a German accent. 'Put it on, get the feel of it,' he pressed.

'How much?' asked Jethro.

'The most important thing is not how much a piece like this costs,' said the store owner, 'it is how it feels. You can buy a cheaper gun and not feel comfortable with it.' He took the Colt and gunbelt out of the window and expertly fastened it round Jethro's waist. 'How does that feel, it is good – no?'

'How much?' repeated Jethro, drawing the gun and weighing it in his hand. He had to admit that it felt very comfortable, but then he had never held such a weapon before so had nothing to judge it by.

'It's not the cheapest,' said Gruber. 'I do have a couple of cheaper ones, but they are not as good or as accurate.'

'How much!?' demanded Jethro again.

'Seventy-five dollars,' came the reply, 'but believe me it would be money well spent.'

'Seventy-five?' mused Jethro. 'What about the others?'

'I have a second-hand Adams but it is only a five shot – this is six – for forty-five dollars,' said Gruber. 'And I have a second-hand DeBrame for the same price, but neither is a match on the Colt.' He opened a cupboard and took out the two pistols and handed them to Jethro who again weighed them as if he were an expert and then cradled the handles in his hand. He had to admit that they did not have quite the same comfortable feel as the Colt.

'Is the Colt new or second-hand?' asked Jethro.

The store owner smiled knowingly. 'A new one would cost much more than seventy-five dollars,' he said. 'I'll tell you what I'll do for you young man. You take the Colt and try it for a few days, if you don't like it I'll take it back and return your money. I cannot say fairer than that, can I?'

Jethro had already been sold on the Colt and nodded. 'OK, I'll take it,' he said. 'I shall be needing some bullets as well.'

'No problem at all,' beamed Hans Gruber who had a knack of knowing when he had made a good sale.

'I haven't got the money on me right now,' said Jethro, 'I'll have to go and get it, I won't be many minutes.'

'The gun will still be here when you return,'

assured Gruber. 'You will not regret your choice.'

'I hope I don't,' said Jethro. 'There's five men who will regret it though, I hope. I'll make no secret of it, I'm only buying a gun like this to kill someone.'

'Apart from men such as the sheriff,' nodded Gruber, 'that is all a man ever buys such a weapon for. What happened to you and your family is known to all in Henderson and everyone understands how you must feel. You are yet a young man who cannot have had a great deal of experience. Have you ever owned or used such a weapon before?' Jethro shook his head. 'I have seen many men handle these guns before,' continued Gruber, 'but as I watched you I felt that you have a natural feel and ability which most men do not possess. You need a few lessons, that is all.'

'And do you know anyone who can give me a few lessons?' asked Jethro, expecting Gruber to offer his services.

'The best man I know is the minister, the Reverend James Gough,' came the rather surprising reply.

'The minister!' exclaimed Jethro disbelievingly.

'*Ja*,' smiled Gruber. 'The Reverend James Gough has not been a man of God all his life. I am one of the few people around here who knew him before he became a priest when he was the Sheriff of Hart County – that is north-east of here. He was well known for being very fast and very accurate with his gun.'

'I saw a sign for Hart way back,' said Jethro, 'where the trail divides and crosses the river. Maybe I was doing the reverend a disservice, I thought he was just one of your regular ministers.'

'There have been others who have also misjudged him,' smiled Gruber, 'as they discovered to their cost.'

'OK,' shrugged Jethro, 'so he's a good gunman. I don't expect he would want to teach me how to use one though.'

'You will never know if you do not ask,' said Gruber, logically.

Having paid for his gun and two boxes of ammunition, Jethro returned to the sheriff's office to show off his new acquisition and to probe the sheriff about the minister. The story was more-or-less the same, Wally agreeing with Hans Gruber that he was certainly the best man to teach anyone how to handle a gun and Jethro decided to at least ask the minister. He fully expected a refusal, but he felt that a refusal would cost him nothing.

'That is a part of my life I try to keep private,' said the reverend when approached by Jethro. 'I suppose it is inevitable that some people know about it, unfortunately. I did consider taking up the ministry in another part of the country, but these lands are where I was born and raised and I do not think I could ever leave.'

'I know it's a lot to ask,' said Jethro, 'and I'll fully understand if you refuse. I guess I could teach myself or get Wally, the sheriff, to help me, but they tell me you are the best and I want to be the best.'

The reverend studied the young man standing before him, giving an outward appearance to the world that he was a man of the world. He nodded and stroked his chin thoughtfully for a few moments.

'Let me see you draw as fast as you can,' he

suddenly said. Jethro was too surprised to draw quickly, even he knew that and he smilingly reholstered his Colt and drew again. This time he was impressively faster. 'Lower your belt a bit,' said the reverend. 'Move it a couple of inches down your hip.' Jethro did as instructed, letting the belt out one hole and retying the thong from the holster round his thigh. The reverend nodded and Jethro drew again, this time finding it much easier.

'You have a natural ability,' said the reverend. 'You will not need much teaching, only plenty of practice. Come back to me this afternoon. Today is Saturday, the one day of the week when all sensible men keep their wives and daughters indoors, the day when people from the outlying farms and the two cattle ranches hit town. Fortunately for me most of them stay overnight and attend service in the morning. I don't think they always do so because they are overly religious, more that they were too drunk on the Saturday to attempt going home. Strangely, from my point of view, it is the one afternoon of the week when I might as well not exist. We can go up to Navaho Creek; very few people ever go up there, especially on a Saturday.'

'Thanks, Reverend!' beamed Jethro. 'I only hope I will be a credit to you.'

'There is no need to thank me,' smiled the minister, 'You must thank my wife. I told her about my fears for you, that you were bent on revenge and it was she who told me that I had to help in whatever way I could. We never had any children, at least none who survived beyond the age of a few months, but she would like to think that had something similar happened to us as happened to you, any son of hers would do exactly the same thing. As a minister I ought to be very disapproving, but I have seen life from the other side and I have shot and killed two men in my previous life so I preach from a standpoint of knowledge and experience. Meet me here at two o'clock and please, do not tell anyone, not even Wally Hutchinson. I am afraid that if you do, we would attract an audience very quickly.' Jethro promised not to say a thing to anyone.

The man Jethro met outside the church at two o'clock was nothing like the man he had met earlier. Gone were the priestly trappings, all replaced by jeans, check shirt, neckerchief, highly polished boots and, worn as though it were perfectly natural, a gunbelt and gun looking very much like the Colt which Jethro had bought. A large and very fine-looking chestnut stallion bearing an ornate saddle gently snorted and tossed its head.

'Your horse,' smiled the reverend. 'Mine is still in the stable.' There were two stables behind the minister's house.

'Mine!' exclaimed Jethro. He had expected to have to ride out to Navaho Creek on a wagon or something. 'You mean I can borrow him for the day, of course.'

'No, I mean he is yours,' smiled the minister. 'Yours to keep. I have little need for him these days and I do have another horse which is slightly more placid. I must admit that he can be quite a handful. My wife has been on at me for a long time to get rid of him, but I didn't like the thought of some farmer buying him and turning him into a working farm horse and the men from the ranches have no feeling at all for their animals.'

Jethro had owned a pony once when he was about fourteen and had always dreamed of owning his own horse, especially one like this. He stroked the animal's nose and was rewarded with a gentle nibbling of his ear with its lips. Both man and horse appeared to strike a rapport at once. Jethro did offer to pay for the animal, which was named Albert, a name which the reverend did not really know why he had adopted, and the offer was refused. The name Albert suited Jethro just fine and a short time later he was riding proudly out of town with the minister.

'You look the part,' smiled the reverend as they rode. 'I can but hope that I am doing the right thing.'

'I won't let you down,' promised Jethro.

'My conscience tells me that by teaching you how to kill, I am letting myself down.'

Jethro proved a very willing and very talented pupil and, by the end of the afternoon, he was drawing and shooting almost as though he had been doing it all his life. He was even becoming quite good at hitting a moving target whilst on the move himself, although by the end of the day the strain on his injured shoulder began to tell on him, even though it had been virtually forgotten throughout the afternoon. They returned to the minister's house just before dusk and Mrs Gough insisted that Jethro have dinner with them, a meal very different from anything he might have expected at Grace's Diner.

In common with most young men, Jethro felt the urge to impress and duly presented himself to Wally

Hutchinson, complete with clean clothes and his new gun, hoping for approval.

'You can take that thing off!' ordered Wally. 'All guns are banned on Saturday night, including shotguns. Anyone found with a gun of any kind gets to spend two days in jail and a twenty-dollar fine.'

'How is a man supposed to defend himself?' asked Jethro, very disappointed.

'By walkin' away from trouble,' said Wally. 'Anyone caught fist fightin' also gets to spend the next two days in jail and a ten-dollar fine and I don't care who the hell they are; even the reverend himself comes in for the same rules. Now take that damned thing off before I lock you away.'

Jethro would have liked to parade around the town, impressing both young ladies and men with his apparent worldliness, but he had to admit that Wally might very well have a problem if he did not enforce the rule. He took off his gun and handed it to Wally who wrote his name on a piece of paper and placed the gun in a pile of others in a corner at the same time as two men came into the office and handed over two rifles to which their names were attached.

'They get them back when they leave town,' explained Wally. 'Most folk don't even bring them in these days, but a few from further out won't leave home without a gun on account of wolves and bears.'

'When can I have mine back?' asked Jethro.

'Son,' said Wally, 'I reckon the best thing you can do with that thing is to leave it here permanently. It won't be safe in your wagon, that's for sure, especially if some tearaway knows you have it. Most folk in these parts don't own one, they're too damned expensive and farmers are notorious for not spending a penny on somethin' they ain't likely to use, but give them a chance of one for nothin' an' they'll take it. You can have it any time you need it, which shouldn't be too often.'

Jethro agreed that the sheriff's office was probably the best place to leave his gun while he was in Henderson. The minister had agreed to keep Albert, his new horse, in his stable until such time as Jethro should leave. He left the office and wandered down to the saloon where he ordered a beer which, very surprisingly when he thought about it, was the first time he had ever ordered a drink on his own.

A few games of cards were taking place and on the far side of the room a large wheel had appeared with a pointer at the top and numbers painted on the wheel on which men were betting as to which number or colour would stop at the pointer. At even money for predicting which colour – red or black – would stop at the pointer, it appeared too easy to the inexperienced Jethro. He took the plunge and placed five dollars on red. He was lucky, it was red which showed and he suddenly found himself five dollars the richer. His next bet, also five dollars, was on black and once again he won. His third bet went on black again and once again he was in pocket, now to the tune of fifteen dollars. His luck held for a fourth time, but when he tried a fifth bet he lost, but he was still fifteen dollars to the good. He was wise enough to stop at that point although he did hang about, watching the wheel and mentally betting and was pleased that he had not bet in reality as his choices went down one after the other. Feeling quite pleased with himself, he ordered another drink and looked about for something to do next.

'I hear you're lookin' fer Pete Watson an' his gang,' a rather scruffy voice said at his side. Jethro looked down to see that the scruffy voice belonged to an equally scruffy, elderly man.

'Could be,' nodded Jethro, trying to appear nonchalant.

'I know where they is,' whispered Scruffy, pressing a little closer. Jethro sniffed the air and wondered where the strange smell was coming from before he realized that Scruffy and the smell were one and the same. 'Buy me a drink an' I'll tell you,' continued Scruffy. 'I've been workin' out on the range for four days an' I ain't had me a decent drink in all that time an' I ain't had me my wages yet. My boss is due to pay me sometime tonight, but he ain't come in yet, an' Jimmy don't allow nobody any credit.' Jethro thought that his boss was a very wise man; if he paid him too soon it would probably be all gone in a very short time.

'A beer for the man,' Jethro said to Jimmy, the bartender. Jimmy smiled knowingly and served the beer. 'Well, I'm waiting,' continued Jethro.

'They is holed up out at Payute Flats,' said Scruffy, after he had drained his glass in one gulp, a feat which seemed quite incredible for such a thin, weedy man. He placed the glass on the counter and looked demandingly at Jethro again. Jethro got the message and ordered another beer for him. This time he did not drink it quite so fast. 'Payute Flats, down by where the river runs into the canyon. There's some caves down there, old Indian caves. That's where they are all right. I know, I seen 'em ride in two days on the trot. They didn't see me; I was supposed to be roundin' up strays, 'ceptin' there warn't none to be seen, so I took it easy.'

'How do you know I want them?' asked Jethro.

'Talk of the town,' smiled Scruffy, once again draining his glass and placing it in front of Jethro. Jethro smiled and paid for another beer and, at a nod from Jimmy, moved along the counter.

'I just thought I'd better warn you,' said Jimmy. 'He tries this on with every stranger. I reckon he gave you the story about workin' on the range an' not havin' been paid yet. . . .' Jethro nodded. 'Sure, he's probably been workin' the range. He makes his livin' roundin' up strays an' sellin' 'em back to their owners. He don't work for nobody but himself.'

'Would he know where Pete Watson was?' asked Jethro.

'More'n like,' nodded Jimmy. 'He's Humpback Chisholm's brother!'

FOUR

'It doesn't make sense,' Jethro said to Jimmy the bartender when he had thought about the information passed on to him by Scruffy Chisholm. 'He just told me where the gang is hiding out, but why should any man want to tell someone where his own brother is if he knows that man is intent on killing the brother?'

'Nothing he does ever makes sense,' replied Jimmy, 'but I do know he ain't as daft as he makes out. The one thing I do know is that him an' his brother hate each other's guts. Don't ask me why, but as far as I know they never even talk to each other, haven't done for years. Why not ask him, it'll probably cost you a few more drinks but it might be worth it?'

Jethro nodded and moved back to where Scruffy Chisholm was trying to prise another beer out of one of the farmers, but, like all farmers, it was very difficult to separate him from his hard won cash. The farmer swore at Scruffy and smiled thinly at Jethro as he joined them, thankful that someone else had arrived to take the attention away from him. He took

51

the opportunity to leave the counter, glass of beer tightly in hand since it was well known that Scruffy would often simply pick up someone else's glass and drink the contents, claiming that he thought it had been abandoned. Jimmy pushed another glass of beer towards Scruffy who took it as though it was the natural thing to do and Jethro tossed a coin to the bartender.

'Your good health, young man,' grinned Scruffy. 'You are a gentleman. There was a time when Henderson was full of gentlemen, but those days have been gone a long time now. Most wouldn't even offer you the drippings off their noses these days.' He scowled at Jimmy as he spoke.

'I wouldn't know about that, I'm fresh from the East,' said Jethro. 'I am curious though. You know I'm looking for the gang led by Pete Watson and that that gang includes Humpback. Why should you want to tell me where they are, I might just kill your brother? In fact, I intend to if I get the chance.'

'Best thing that could happen to the bastard!' said Scruffy, slurping through his beer. 'He might be my brother but that don't mean I've got to like him. I had nothin' to do with his arrival in the world; in fact, it was a question of who arrived first, but I guess that hump of his must've held him up. We always disliked each other as kids, but then I know of plenty of other brothers who don't like each other an' I don't go along with all that crap about blood bein' thicker'n water.'

'It doesn't necessarily mean that you would want to see him dead either,' said Jethro. 'Why did you tell me?'

'It's a long story, son,' muttered Scruffy. 'All you

need to know is that as far as I'm concerned he ain't no brother of mine. The long an' short of it is he ended up rapin' an' murderin' my wife an' daughter. Imagine that, rapin' an' murderin' your own flesh an' blood.'

'So why wasn't he hanged or sent to prison?' asked Jethro.

'That's 'cos nobody could ever prove nothin',' muttered Scruffy. 'Just like they ain't never been able to prove nothin' about the other things they've done since. I was in prison myself at the time, so there was nothin' I could do an' it seems like the law just didn't want to know. He never made any secret of it, least-ways not to me. In fact he used to gloat about it.'

'So why haven't you killed him yourself?'

Scruffy held up his hands which were badly twisted. 'Look at these! I ain't sure who came off worse, me or him. He's allus had the hump on his back an' I've allus had twisted hands. Don't know why we should've been born like it, but we were. Some folk say it was 'cos we must have been evil in a previous life, but I don't go for that stuff. Me an' Humpback are what they call twins 'ceptin' we don't really look like each other. Anyhow, my ma always insisted that we was born on the same day so I guess that makes us twins. My ma used to reckon I was older'n him by about half an hour.'

'Did either of your parents suffer from anything like this?' asked Jethro, indicating Scruffy's deformed hands. The hands were held up and Scruffy made a show of trying to move his fingers. He finally gave up, but Jethro did notice that those same fingers had little difficulty in grasping the glass of beer.

'My ma sure didn't,' laughed Scruffy. 'Only thing she ever suffered from was a bad back, but then she was hardly ever off it since she had a man between her legs most of the time. Don't know about my pa. I never knew him an' I don't think even my ma knew who he was.' He drained his glass and placed it meaningfully in front of Jethro who took the hint and paid for another. 'You an' me got one thing in common,' grinned Scruffy, 'we'd both like to see my brother dead. I ain't got no argument against the other four, leastways not so far as I know, but it sure wouldn't bother me none if they was killed, they is all as bad as each other. I can't do it myself, I can't hold a gun properly. I've tried more'n once, but it just don't work. By the time I'd manage to take aim even a new-born baby could have the drop on me.'

'But I can,' nodded Jethro. 'You want to use me to avenge your wife and daughter.'

'That's about the size of it,' nodded Scruffy. 'I'll do a deal with you, young feller. I'll lead you to 'em an' you kill 'em, but just make sure you kill that so-called brother of mine first.'

'I'm not a gunman,' said Jethro. 'Until today I had never even held a pistol.'

'You looked pretty good to me,' smiled Scruffy. 'I was watchin' you an' the priest gettin' in some practice up at Navaho Creek this mornin'. You couldn't find a better teacher anywhere, I knew him when he was a sheriff an' he was the best I'd ever seen then. I never did understand why he quit that job an' took up religion. Anyhow, I hear tell you survived Doc Galloway an' anyone who pulls through as fast as you seem to have done after bein' cut up by that drunkard must be pretty damned fit or very lucky, or maybe both.'

'You were up at Navaho Creek?' said Jethro. 'I didn't see you and I'm sure the minister didn't. Anyhow, you seem to be running Doc Galloway a close second when it comes to drinking.'

'But I don't have to cut into folk,' grinned Scruffy. 'I might not be very pretty to look at, but I can blend into the landscape better'n most men. I see a hell of a lot of things too. I know which farmer's screwin' which other farmer's wife or daughter an' even a couple of farmers who is screwin' each other.' He laughed. 'Sure, I know a lot of things about a lot of folk an' occasionally I use it to get somethin' I want, but I wouldn't tell nobody nothin' but they don't know that. Anyhow, what about it, young feller, I help you an' you help me?'

'You've got a deal,' said Jethro leaping in before he had really given it any thought. 'You lead me to them an' I'll do the rest.'

'All I can say is if you succeed you'd better just keep on ridin',' warned Sheriff Wally Hutchinson. 'It sounds to me like cold-blooded murder an' I'd have to arrest you. The only chance you'd have is if I never found the bodies an' you rode on. You ain't the first one Sam Chisholm has tried to get to do his dirty work. He uses the excuse of his hands to get other folk to do all kinds of things, but he can use 'em if he needs to.'

'Cold-blooded murder!' exclaimed Jethro. 'What about what they did to my folk? If anythin' was cold-blooded that was.'

'You bring me one scrap of proof which would stand up in a court of law an' I'll arrest 'em,' said Wally. 'Sure, you know what you saw an' what you heard, but any half-baked lawyer could pull that story to pieces very easily.'

'What more proof do you want?' demanded Jethro angrily. 'Seems to me that Scruffy was right. . . .'

'Scruffy?' interrupted Wally.

'Yes, Sam Chisholm,' said Jethro, the anger rising in him. 'I just sort of christened him Scruffy an' I prefer it to his given name, it suits him better. Anyhow, whatever you call him, he was right when he said the law just didn't seem interested in what happened to his wife and daughter and I'm beginning to think you don't really care about what happened to my family. Sure, you've been a good friend to me since I've been here and I appreciate it, but I'm starting to think that all any of you want is a peaceful life, justice just doesn't seem to interest any of you.'

'I'm hurt, son,' said Wally. 'I would have thought that as someone recently from the East where they have different kinds of lawmen from what I hear an' where they're supposed to have a better system, that you would've appreciated I can't act without some proof.' Jethro immediately felt sorry for his outburst and apologized. 'All I'm tryin' to tell you, son, is be careful, don't do nothin' stupid an' make sure I can't arrest you for anythin'.'

'I won't,' assured Jethro. 'Anyhow, I've arranged to meet Scruffy up at Navaho Creek just after dawn on Monday. He's taking me out to some place called Payute Flats and some caves.'

'I know 'em,' said Wally. 'I heard they were hidin' out there. Perfect place too, almost impossible to get close.'

'The one thing that does puzzle me is why do they

need to hide out?' said Jethro. 'If you haven't been able to prove anything against them, why the need to act like they're outlaws?'

Wally smiled. 'That's easy,' he said. 'Where they are is just inside the state border. I know they're wanted in other states, but not here. They use the caves to cross the border and do whatever they want to do and they won't take the risk on me arrestin' 'em and handin' 'em over. They have been told I can't do that without what they call an extradition warrant and so far nobody has taken one out.'

'Well, I intend to change all that,' said Jethro. 'If it means I have to follow them across the border, then that's what I'll do.'

'But your folk were killed in this state,' Wally pointed out.

Jethro shook his head sadly. 'It's all too complicated for me,' he sighed. 'I'll just have to play things as I go along.'

'Just you take care,' advised Wally.

Dawn on Monday morning out at Navaho Creek was rather cold and overcast, threatening rain, something of a rarity since the rainy season was not due for at least another month, but Scruffy Chisholm assured Jethro that it was not going to rain and that such starts to the day were not at all unusual.

'It'll take about two hours to reach the caves,' said Scruffy. 'Leastways it takes my old mule that long; that fine horse of yours could probably do it in half the time.'

'I'm in no great hurry,' assured Jethro. 'In fact I am beginning to wonder if this is such a good idea after all.'

'Gettin' cold feet!' grinned Scruffy. 'Don't worry son, from what I've seen you can outdraw any of 'em.'

'It wasn't that I meant,' said Jethro. 'I was starting to think it might be better to let them come to me, that way I might be able to deal with them and not stand accused of murder.'

'They killed your folks,' Scruffy pointed out.

'That don't mean that if I kill them in cold blood it isn't murder on my part,' said Jethro.

'You've been talkin' to Wally Hutchinson,' said Scruffy. 'He's a good man, probably the best sheriff Henderson ever had, but he's a bit of a stickler for doin' things by the book.'

'Is that wrong?' asked Jethro.

'No, nothin' wrong with it at all,' nodded Scruffy. 'Only trouble with that is the book was written by folk back East who don't know how the West really works. Sometimes the only way to get justice is to take the law into your own hands.'

'They call it lynching, don't they?' said Jethro.

'Sometimes,' agreed Scruffy. 'Anyhow, you make your mind up, son. Either we ride out to Payute Canyon right now or we go back to town an' forget the whole thing.'

Jethro had in fact been considering that question most of the night and certainly that morning as he had ridden out to Navaho Creek, but despite any misgivings he might still have, the prospect of avenging his parents and sister proved too strong to resist. He nodded and the pair crossed the shallow Navaho Creek and slowly headed north towards Payute Flats.

Scruffy Chisholm's assessment of how long it would take to reach Payute Flats proved to be very accurate.

Jethro had checked the time on the pocket watch he had taken from his father's body, when they had crossed the Navaho Creek and it was exactly two hours later when Scruffy stopped behind a group of large boulders and pointed down at a large, flat, salty-looking plain stretching away to the east as far as they could see, westward to a range of mountains perhaps ten miles away and north towards a ridge of cliffs which stretched almost from the mountains to about halfway to the distant horizon across the plain. A river snaked its way across the plain and seemed to disappear into the cliff face.

'Payute Flats,' announced Scruffy, stating the obvious. 'The river there runs into Payute Canyon, that's where the caves are.'

'That must be about five miles,' said Jethro. 'It's all open country too; how the hell do we get close without being seen?'

Scruffy laughed. 'Leave that to your Uncle Sam,' he said. 'From here it does look pretty flat an' for the most part it is, but there's a lot of channels an' gullies you can't make out from here. When it rains the gullies fill up an' sometimes, when it rains really heavy, the whole of Payute Flats turns into a lake. That's why it's salty; when it does flood the water just gets soaked up by the sun an' leaves the salt behind. Anyhow, some of them are deep enough so that you can't be seen, an' I know 'em all; I ought to, I've used 'em often enough.'

'Then I guess I'm in your hands,' said Jethro. He checked that both his new Colt and his rifle were fully loaded and that he had some spare ammunition slotted into his belt. When he was ready he nodded to his guide and they started off down the deceptively steep slope to the plain.

At first Scruffy seemed content to cross the plain without resorting to the many gullies, but when they were about halfway he dropped down into one of the deepest gullies, which at first seemed to take them away from the caves and the canyon, but which later swung round to the right direction. Once or twice they rode up the steep slopes to give themselves a better view of what lay ahead. Eventually, Scruffy led the way out of the gully and across a short, rock-covered stretch of land where the only cover they had was provided by the many large rocks. They finally ended up below the cliff, which at that point rose about 200 feet sheer.

'The canyon starts about a mile along there,' said Scruffy, pointing eastwards, 'an' the caves are just this side of the canyon. From here on in, it gets more difficult to keep out of sight.'

'So how do I get close enough?' asked Jethro, once again beginning to wonder if he had made the right decision. 'It seems to me the cards are all stacked in their favour. Anyhow, we don't even know if they're there. Another thing is that we make a pretty odd-looking couple. They probably know who you and your mule are but they don't know me. If things are as you say they are between your brother and you, they might work it out that we are in this together.'

'You stay here, son,' nodded Scruffy. 'I'm in these parts regular enough so they won't think anythin's wrong. I'll just check to see if they're still there.'

Jethro dismounted and led his horse over to a patch of rough grass and watched as Scruffy and his mule slowly meandered between the boulders and

were eventually lost from sight. He took the opportunity to clamber part way up the cliff face to give
himself a better view of his surroundings and was
rather surprised to see a fairly large pool of clear
water between where he was and the canyon and,
judging by the fact that there appeared to be some
ducks swimming around, he assumed that it was not
salty as Scruffy had warned him nearly all the other
pools were. The previously cloudy, threatening sky
had slowly given way to bright, hot sunlight, the
clouds apparently having miraculously dissolved. He
would have liked to have taken his horse, Albert,
down to the pool, but he thought that he had better
wait until Scruffy returned.

It was about half an hour later, which struck Jethro
as being quite a long time for the distance involved,
when Scruffy and his mule plodded into view and
Scruffy seemed slightly annoyed. 'Only one of 'em
there,' he announced. 'Curly Johnson. He saw me
an' he even waved to me, but I didn't go too close.
Anyhow, the others are off somewhere. I was kinda
hopin' to get 'em all together.'

Jethro actually felt quite relieved that they were
not together. As comfortable as he felt with his new
gun, he had yet to face a human being and he had
been warned often enough that it was one thing to
shoot game or at a target and something totally
different to actually place a man in the sights and
squeeze the trigger. In that respect though, he knew
that he had no problems, but only having to face one
man would make life that much easier and he
intended facing Curly Johnson. His one ambition in
life at that moment was to avenge the death of his
parents and sister and he was not prepared to miss

any opportunity.

'You stay here,' he said to Scruffy. 'I'll go in alone. As far as I know none of them ever actually saw me and they certainly won't be expecting me to be riding a horse like Albert here. Now, give me some idea of the layout.'

Scruffy took a stick and drew outlines in the dirt, pointing out various large rocks and exactly where the caves were. There were apparently four large caves, one at ground level which they used to stable their horses and the others about fifteen feet up the cliff, but with easy access to all three. Scruffy appeared uncertain as to which cave they actually occupied although he seemed to think that it was the one nearest the canyon. Once again Jethro went through the routine of checking his guns, although he had done that at least twice since leaving Navaho Creek and he then remounted his horse.

'If you hear shooting and I'm not back within about half an hour, you'd better assume that I've been killed,' he said.

'I reckon I'll see you back,' grinned Scruffy. Jethro nodded and spurred Albert onwards.

His idea was to act as though he were simply another traveller passing through and to this end he stopped by the pool of water for some time, while Albert drank his flll and he too quenched his thirst. From the pool he could see the three caves set up in the cliff, although he did not see the man Scruffy had mentioned. After what seemed to him a reasonable time, he remounted and wandered slowly closer to the caves. As he approached, he had the feeling that he was being watched and his hand automatically went to his gunbelt and gently eased the Colt to make it looser and easier to draw. He also casually eased his rifle in the saddle holster.

He saw the horse long before he saw the man and, pretending an interest in the horse, he moved closer to the caves. The horse was grazing on the rough grass and at first there was no sign of Curly Johnson, but when he was about twenty yards from the lower cave a voice suddenly rasped out behind him.

'Hold it right there, mister!' came the command. Jethro turned to see a man standing on a large rock with a rifle pointing directly him.

'It's getting so's a man can't get away from anyone,' smiled Jethro, making no attempt to go for his Colt since he knew that the man was beyond its range and any attempt to remove his rifle would be a waste of time.

'What you talkin' about?' demanded Curly Johnson.

'I just met some old tramp of a feller back there and now I meet you,' laughed Jethro, doing his best to appear casual. 'How many more are there?'

'Only me for the moment,' replied Curly. 'What you doin' here?'

'Just making my way through,' said Jethro. 'Minding my own business and making my way through, that's all.'

'Where to?' demanded Curly again.

'That I don't know,' shrugged Jethro. 'Wherever the fancy takes me I suppose. Is there any law against that or am I trespassing on somebody's land? If I am I didn't see any signs saying so.'

Curly jumped down from the rock and briefly Jethro was tempted to draw his gun but something told him it was not yet time. Curly slowly approached

Jethro and looked questioningly at both him and
Albert, his horse.

'I've seen that horse somewhere before,' he said
suspiciously, raising his rifle slightly. 'The one thing I
do know about is horseflesh an' I never forget a good
horse when I see it. Where'd you get this animal,
feller?' The rifle was now aimed at Jethro's chest.
Jethro thought quickly and decided to tell the truth,
or at least part of it, enough hopefully to allay Curly's
suspicions.

'I bought it back in Henderson,' explained Jethro,
'from the local minister as a matter of fact. My horse
had gone lame and the minister offered to sell him
to me.' This explanation seemed to have the effect of
making Curly even more suspicious.

'Sure, it's his horse all right,' he said, lowering the
rifle very slightly. 'I'd know him anywhere. I wanted
to buy him from the minister myself, but he always
said he'd never sell. OK, so why has he suddenly
decided to sell to a complete stranger?'

'How the hell should I know that?' challenged
Jethro. 'You don't think I stole him or murdered the
minister or something, do you?'

'I ain't sure what I think,' said Curly. 'Thinkin'
ain't my strongest point, but I do know when somethin' don't smell right an' this is one time it stinks.
Drop your gun an' get down. I'm goin' to hold you
until Pete an' the others get back, he'll know what to
do about you.'

'And when will that be?' asked Jethro. 'I can't
afford to wait too long.'

'Go shit!' spat Curly. 'You just said you was just
passin' through an' you ain't tied to time, you can
wait as long as it takes. Now, throw that gun down an'

get off that horse before I forget myself an' shoot you off it.'

Jethro smiled, sighed and casually took the Colt out of his holster as he started to dismount. He knew that he had now about one second to put into practice all that the Reverend James Gough had taught him about moving and shooting at the same time.

It all happened so quickly that Jethro was never certain as to exactly what he did do. He vaguely remembered crashing to the ground and firing his Colt whilst still in mid air. Whatever he did he must have done something right because his shot shattered into Curly's shoulder, making his drop the rifle. Fortunately for Jethro, the injured shoulder was on the side Curly wore his handgun and before he could reach it with his other hand, Jethro was up and standing over him, his Colt trained at Curly's head.

'I'm glad I didn't kill you straight away,' gloated Jethro. 'Before you die, Mr Curly Johnson – yes, I know who you are – before you die, I just want you to know who I am. I guess you must've thought I was dead too. A few days ago you raped an' murdered my mother and sister and murdered my father. . . .' A look of terror came into Curly's face. 'I see you know who I'm talking about. I was the son, the one who shot one of you. You should have checked that I was dead, it would have saved you a lot of bother.'

'That was Pete an' Humpback!' croaked Curly, his hand clasped to his injured shoulder. 'I didn't touch either your mother or your sister an' it was Humpback who killed your father. . . . Don't shoot, honest, it wasn't me.'

'I'm sorry, I don't believe you,' snarled Jethro.

'Not that it's going to do either of us much good, I just wanted you to know who I was before I killed you.'

'No . . . please, no,' grovelled Curly, trying to drag himself away. 'It wasn't. . . .'

He never did complete his sentence as, quite coldly, deliberately and very calmly, Jethro squeezed the trigger. . . .

FIVE

Falling off his horse had not done Jethro's shoulder any good at all, the wound had started to bleed again and at first Scruffy thought that he had been shot, but examination of the wound indicated that a couple of stitches had broken. Jethro packed it with his neckerchief and decided that he had better let Doc Galloway take a look at it as soon as he returned to Henderson.

'What about Curly?' asked Scruffy. 'Are you just goin' to leave him there?'

'There doesn't seem to be a lot of point in doing anything else,' said Jethro. 'At least the others might get the message.'

'Get the message?' queried Scruffy. 'Do you want 'em to know who killed him?'

'Why not?' grinned Jethro. 'If they come after me it'll save me a lot of bother and it'll look better when I kill them.'

'But they won't know who did it or why,' Scruffy pointed out.

'That's where you come in,' grinned Jethro. 'You tell them who I am.'

'An' get myself killed for leadin' you out here!'
objected Scruffy. 'I ain't into committin' suicide.'

'You don't have to tell them anything,' said Jethro.
'All you have to do is ride out here, in the morning
say, pretend you don't know a thing about Curly
being dead but mention that it could possibly be me.
Say something like you met me in town or you'd
heard about me and that I was looking for them. You
can tell them about me buying the horse off the
minister. That ought to make them do something.
You want to see your brother dead just as much as I
do, so how I do it shouldn't bother you too much and
I don't suppose for one moment you give a damn if I
get myself killed or not.'

'How you do it sure don't bother me,' said Scruffy.
'I just think tellin' 'em about it is about as close to
suicide as a man can get.'

'It's my suicide,' grinned Jethro.

When they reached Henderson, the pain in Jethro's
shoulder was quite severe and the first thing he did
was to go round to Doc Galloway who peered at the
wound and announced that he had better insert two
more stitches and he did not give Jethro the opportunity to object or refuse. Jethro was uncertain which
was the most painful, the broken stitches or having
the new ones inserted. However, he gritted his teeth,
sweated profusely and tried not to shout in pain. He
did not actually shout, but he certainly made his
discomfort known.

Sheriff Wally Hutchinson asked no questions,
although it was obvious that he knew something had
happened. He appeared to be working on the prin-
ciple that if nobody complained or reported

anything, he did not know anything. Jethro
wondered what the chances were of the gang report-
ing the death to the sheriff, although talking to
Scruffy on the way back, he had been assured that
they would not dare to say anything and even if they
did, nobody, including Wally Hutchinson, would be
in any way interested or otherwise concerned. Jethro
was not at all certain as to what the sheriff's reaction
would be and, if only for the sheriff's sake, he did not
want to put him to the test.

Albert, his new horse, was stabled in the Reverend
James Gough's stable, Jethro having been told that
he was free to use it all the time he was in
Henderson. When he went along to the stable on his
return, neither the minister or his wife were at home.
For some strange reason Jethro felt bound to tell the
minister what had happened even if nobody else was
told. After partaking of another very indifferent meal
of beef stew and stodgy dumplings – the dumplings
having the advantage of filling him up if nothing else
– at Grace's place, he returned to the minister's
house. This time both the minister and his wife were
at home and appeared genuinely pleased to see him.
Neither of them made any comment when he told
them what had happened. In fact, Mrs Gough
seemed almost pleased, but the reverend put on a
severe face as he poured out a large measure of
good, Scotch whisky and handed it to Jethro.

'I said I was never going to touch whisky again,' he
said, holding up the glass and looking at it dubiously.

'This is not a bit like Jimmy's special,' smiled the
minister. 'This is the best money can buy, imported
all the way from Scotland, the only place where they
really know how to make it. Even if it doesn't say

Scotch on the bottle, you can usually tell if it is Scotch or not simply by the way they spell whisky. The way the Scottish people spell it there is no "e", everyone else spells it with an "e".' He pointed out the word whisky on the bottle.

Jethro said something about not being a regular drinker of it and he had therefore never thought about the spelling and, in his opinion, all the whisky he had ever tasted was an experience similar to drinking broken glass. He did modify his opinion slightly when he tasted the whisky handed to him, likening it to rather more finely ground glass.

'Was I wrong?' Jethro asked, as both men settled on the verandah with their glasses.

'Do you believe you were wrong?' replied the minister.

'No!' said Jethro, firmly. 'My folk deserved something more than just being given a proper burial. For them their dream ended through no fault of their own and the greed and evil of others. Why should those who committed such a crime be allowed to get away with it?'

'We have laws about such things,' said the reverend.

'Sure, I know that,' nodded Jethro, 'and believe me I would be the first to turn to the law, but occasionally, so it seems to me, the law is like a bear with no claws or teeth, it can't really do much except stand there and roar.'

'I know exactly what you mean,' nodded the minister. He looked at Jethro and smiled. 'Not many people know this, but we had a son once, in fact he would have been exactly your age. He was murdered by a gang of outlaws when they robbed a bank in

Hart – that's where I used to be sheriff. He was only twelve years old, just like any other twelve-year-old boy who just happened to be in the wrong place at the wrong time. Anyway, one of them shot him as they made their getaway. Fortunately he died instantly, but as far as I was concerned he had been murdered in cold blood. I knew the identity of the man who killed him and vowed to take revenge. I managed to track the man down about six months later, but by that time he was a very sick man and in a sorry state. It was obvious that he was close to death and, even though I could have killed him quite easily and without anyone finding out, I took pity on him and let him live what little time I thought he had. That was a mistake: two days after I had had my chance, he robbed a general store and killed the store owner and his wife. True, he was shot and killed as he left the store, but the point was that had I taken my chance two days earlier, those two people would have still been alive. I never forgave myself for that and I have always blamed myself for the deaths of two innocent people.'

'Is that why you became a minister?' asked Jethro.

'It's part of it,' he agreed. He studied Jethro again for a few moments and then nodded. 'She's right,' he said eventually. Jethro looked puzzled but said nothing. 'My wife says that had Clem – our son – lived, he would have looked exactly like you. I suppose what I am really trying to say is that I hope you succeed in tracking down and killing those men. I know that as a man of God I should try to make you turn the other cheek, but after my experience with my son's killer, I feel it is only right that these men be stopped before they kill others.' He smiled and laughed lightly. "Vengeance is mine, said the Lord". That may be true, but I do believe that there are occasions when the hand of God needs pointing in the right direction. As for the law, I am afraid, speaking from experience, that there are occasions when the law is powerless. The law requires proof and there is nothing wrong with that, but sometimes the law, too, needs pointing in the right direction.'

'That makes me feel easier,' said Jethro quietly. 'I was always brought up to respect the church and I have been a regular church-goer all my life and I was a bit worried about the way I felt when I killed that man. I can't say that I actually enjoyed doing it, but I certainly didn't mind and I definitely do not feel any guilt and I am quite certain that I would do exactly the same thing again, given the opportunity.'

'Does Wally Hutchinson know?' asked the minister.

'I think he does,' nodded Jethro. 'I haven't actually told him how or who but he knows something happened out at Payute Flats, but he's not asking any questions because I think he'd rather not know just in case he might have to arrest me.'

'He'll have to know sometime,' said the minister.

'I guess so,' nodded Jethro, 'but I'll worry about that when the time comes.'

Scruffy Chisholm had the distinct feeling that he had managed to get himself involved in something in which he was completely out of his depth, a feeling reinforced as four men surrounded him, all with guns aimed at him and all seemingly ready to shoot.

'So who killed Curly?' demanded Pete Watson. 'You seem to know almost everythin' what's goin' on.'

'I . . . I don't know,' faltered Scruffy. 'I wasn't out this way yesterday.'

'Go shit!' barked Humpback Chisholm, Scruffy's twin brother. 'I knows you well enough to know when you is lyin', Sam. Curly was murdered here yesterday an' you know more about it than you is admittin'.'

'Why should I know anythin'?' wailed Sam, alias Scruffy. 'It sure wasn't me, if that's what you're thinkin'.'

'That I do believe,' hissed Humpback. 'You'd never have the guts to do anythin' like that. It was always the same when we was kids, it was always me what ended up doin' the dirty work an' usually gettin' the blame for it as well.'

Although Scruffy had gone back to Payute Flats, as agreed with Jethro Smith, he had realized that he had been an accomplice and knew that should Pete or his brother, Humpback, find out, they would certainly kill him. It had all seemed so simple when Jethro had told him what to do, but suddenly faced with the reality, it all looked so very different.

'We don't like it when folk tell us lies,' threatened Clubfoot Higgins. 'Especially when his name is Chisholm – Sam Chisholm.'

'I ain't lyin'!' wailed Scruffy.

'Yes you is!' grated Humpback. 'You smell when you're lyin'.' He laughed loudly. 'Christ knows you smell bad enough any time, but when you is lyin' you always give off some other smell. I can't say what it is an' I don't think nobody but me would notice it, but it was allus the same when we was kids. Ma could smell it too. I could allus rely on you to give the game away an' get us both a damned good beatin' if not from Ma then from whoever she was livin' with at the time.'

Scruffy licked his lips and gulped. 'Maybe it was that new feller in town,' he said hoarsely. 'I hear his folks were murdered in their wagon. His ma, pa an' sister.'

'New feller?' rasped Pete, looking at the others. 'How old?'

'I'd say about twenty,' said Scruffy, wiping the sweat from his forehead. 'The story is that he was shot too, but he survived an' now he's out lookin' for vengeance. I hear tell that he bought the minister's horse.'

'It can't be,' said Ernie Price to the others. 'He was dead, we saw his body.'

'But we never went down to check,' reminded Pete. 'It could be him.' He snarled at Scruffy, 'If it is the same feller, he was definitely injured. You say this feller was shot, where?'

'Word is that he was,' nodded Scruffy. 'Left shoulder, so they tell me. Anyhow, he had to be operated on by Doc Galloway.' The four men looked at each other and nodded.

'Somethin' don't sit right with me,' hissed Humpback. 'I know you almost as well as I know myself, Sam. Somethin' tells me you know a hell of a lot more than you're lettin' on. For instance, how the hell did he know who we are and where to find us? The only person who knows where we are is you. You put him on to us, didn't you, Sam?' He raised his gun to his brother's head. 'You got ten seconds to start tellin' the truth. . . .'

'He . . . I hear tell that he heard your names before you killed his folk,' sweated Scruffy.

'Yeh, maybe he did,' conceded Pete Watson. 'I suppose we must've called each other's names an' he

was outside the wagon for a time, exactly how long
we don't know. OK, so maybe that explains how he
knew who we were,' he continued, 'but that don't
explain how he knew where we were. Humpy's right;
I reckon it was you who pointed him this way. We all
know you'd like to see your brother dead.'

'I'd say you not only told him how to find us,' said
Ernie Price, 'I reckon you brought him out here as
well.'

'No . . . no . . .' gasped Scruffy, knowing full well
that none of them would have any qualms about
killing him. 'I ain't even met the feller, honest I
ain't.'

'You're lyin'!' snarled Humpback. 'You're startin'
to smell again.'

'No, no I'm not!' grovelled Scruffy. 'I've told you
everythin' I know, honest I have.'

'That's easy to check,' said Pete Watson. 'All we
have to do ask Jimmy from the saloon, he knows
everythin' that's goin' on.' Scruffy looked wild-eyed
and Pete sensed his unease. 'OK, tell you what we do.
We keep you here while we check. If you're clean you
can go, but if we find out you've been tellin' us lies,
then you die. Do you understand, Sam?' Scruffy
nodded and gulped. 'Right, I suggest that Ernie an'
me ride into Henderson an' find out what we can.
Clubfoot, you an' Humpy stay here with this scum-
bag.' Everyone agreed to this and Scruffy was
bundled off to one of the caves.

'If this feller knows who we are,' Ernie pointed
out, 'ain't we takin' a risk goin' into town? Not that
I'm scared or anythin', but he might just try an' kill
us.'

'He can try,' grinned Pete. 'We leave it to him to

make the first move, that way we can claim it was self-defence when we kill him.'

The whole of Henderson was on the alert as Pete Watson and Ernie Price were sighted about two miles out of town. Most people suddenly discovered that they had very important business elsewhere and by the time the two men rode along the main street, there were no more than half-a-dozen people about and one of these was Wally Hutchinson, the sheriff. Jethro Smith was, at that moment, with Doc Galloway having his wound attended to. The two men ignored the sheriff who was sitting outside his office and rode down to where the wagon would have been laid up, behind the sawmill, since they knew that was where all the settlers' wagons were directed when they passed through.

'That sure looks like the same wagon to me,' said Ernie.

'And me,' agreed Pete Watson. 'It looks like we got ourselves a feller hell bent on killin' us. Now all we got to do is find him an' kill him before he can kill us.'

'What about Sam?' asked Ernie.

'We go talk to Jimmy,' said Pete.

Jimmy proved singularly dumb, simply grunting in answer to their questions although he did confirm that Scruffy Chisholm had been in the bar on Saturday evening and had tried his usual trick of cadging free drinks off the newcomer. As far as Pete and Ernie were concerned, this proved that Scruffy had been lying. Sheriff Wally Hutchinson came into the room and stood alongside the pair.

'It ain't often we're honoured with your presence

in town,' said the sheriff. 'I somehow don't think this is entirely a social visit though. What was so interestin' down by the sawmill?'

'Nothin' in particular,' said Pete. 'There ain't no law against it, is there?'

'Probably not,' nodded Wally. 'So what brings you into town?'

'Our horses!' grinned Ernie.

'Don't try the funnies on me,' snapped Wally. 'Since you are here, I'd like to ask you a few questions and I want some straight answers.'

'Do we have a choice?' asked Pete.

'Not if you want to stay out of jail,' said Wally. 'OK, I'll start with your obvious interest in the covered wagon behind the mill. I get the impression that you were checkin' on it for some reason. Could it be that you've seen it before somewhere?' Both men shook their heads in denial. Wally grunted and tapped his fingers on the counter for a few moments. 'Three folk were murdered in that wagon,' he continued. 'I don't suppose you'd know anythin' about that either?' Once again they shook their heads. 'Strange that,' he said. 'There's a young feller in town who is willin' to swear on oath that the men who murdered his folks an' sister were called Pete Watson, Ernie Price, Clubfoot Higgins, Curly Johnson and Humpback Chisholm.'

'Then there must be other folk by those names,' said Pete.

'Not in these parts there ain't,' said Wally. 'Anyhow, you tell me where he got them names from, he's fresh from the East an' don't know nobody out West.'

'How the hell should we know that?' said Pete

Watson. 'More'n like he talked to some farmer who suggested us, we know we have somethin' of a reputation.'

'Sure, you've got a reputation an' it's well earned,' said Wally, knowing that what they said could be argued in court by any average lawyer. 'So far you've managed to keep out of my jail, but I have the feelin' that pretty soon now you'll either end up there or dead. Personally I'd prefer it if you did end up dead, it'd save me an' everyone else a whole load of trouble.'

'Curly is already dead,' said Ernie Price, 'an' we reckon it was this new feller you got in town who killed him. You ought to be arrestin' him for murder.'

'Curly!' grunted Wally. At least it confirmed something he had suspected. 'Well, I guess that's one down an' four to go.'

'Are you goin' to let him get away with it?' demanded Pete Watson.

'Tell you what,' laughed Wally, 'you confess to the murder of them folk in the wagon an' I'll arrest him for the murder of Curly. I can't say fairer'n that, can I?'

'We don't know nothin' about no wagon or who murdered 'em,' said Pete, 'but we do have Curly's body if you want proof.'

'And I got the bodies of the three folk murdered in the wagon,' said Wally. 'The fact that Curly is dead don't prove a thing. For all I know you could have had a row an' ended up killin' him yourself.'

'OK, you made your point,' sighed Pete. 'It looks to me like there's one law for some an' one law for folk like us. We've got the reputation so we must be guilty. I hear this stranger an' Sam Chisholm is kinda friendly. Sam told us about him this mornin'.'

'He tried bummin' a drink off him,' confirmed Wally, 'but that's about all as far as I know. Now, I run a pretty clean town an' folk like you in it kinda spoils things for the rest. I suggest you drink up, do whatever business you have to an' leave. Whatever happens I want you out of town by noon at the latest. If you're still around after then I'll throw you in jail an' maybe forget where I put the key.'

'We're on our way,' said Pete Watson. 'I guess we've done all the business we need to, for the moment. Just one thing, Sheriff, you tell this feller, whatever his name is. . . .'

'Jethro Smith,' interrupted Wally.

'Yeh, well you tell this Jethro Smith,' continued Pete, 'that we know he killed Curly an' that as long as he remains within a hundred miles of Henderson, he just might meet with a fatal accident, an' that could go for anyone who tries to help him.'

'Is that a threat?' smiled Wally.

'Let's just call it a warnin',' grated Pete. 'There's some rugged country out there an' it's surprisin' how easy it is for a horse to lose its footin' an' throw a rider.'

'I'll see to it that he gets the message,' said Wally. He left the saloon and almost immediately met Jethro. He quickly pulled him into an alleyway and indicated that he keep quiet. His action was not altogether prompted by the thought that Jethro might try to kill the other two, but more by a desire to avoid trouble. He peered round the corner and saw Pete and Ernie mount their horses and then motioned Jethro to look. 'See them two,' he whispered. 'Pete

Watson and Ernie Price. . . .' He clamped Jethro's hand firmly as he went for his gun. 'Not now!' he warned. 'This is my town an' you'll do as 1 say unless you want to end up in jail charged with the murder of Curly Johnson.' Jethro growled something but relaxed and studied the two men.

'At least I know who I'm looking for,' he said, as they rode away.

'An' they know who they're lookin' for,' said Wally. They stepped out into the main street and watched the riders disappear. 'You never told me about Curly Johnson,' he said. 'Why didn't you tell me?'

'You never asked,' smiled Jethro. 'I had the feeling that you didn't really want to know.'

'I guess not,' sighed the sheriff. 'The thing is, now I do know. They claim Curly was murdered. Tell me that ain't true, tell me he was killed in a fair fight.'

'He was killed in a fair fight,' confirmed Jethro.

'That makes me feel much better,' Wally sighed again. Actually he believed that it probably had been a fair fight.

'The Reverend Gough knows all about it,' said Jethro. 'I had to tell him if I never told anyone else.'

'Sort of confession,' smiled Wally. 'I won't bother to ask him; no minister worth the name would tell about somethin' said in confession.'

'It wasn't in confess—'

'Like I said,' interrupted Wally, 'Confessionals are secret. Now, have you seen Sam Chisholm about?'

'Scruffy? No,' said Jethro, finally grasping the point the sheriff was trying to make. 'He did say he was riding out to Payute Flats this morning though.'

'And that's what he must've done,' said Wally. 'I have the feelin' that we might never see Sam

Chisholm in these parts again. I can't say that I'm all that bothered what happens to him; he sure won't be missed by nobody, not even the ranchers whose stray cattle he rounds up and charges two dollars a head for. If he did suddenly disappear they might find that they don't get quite so many strays. They know that he ain't averse to cuttin' a few head out of a herd now an' then an' claimin' he found 'em out on the plains, but they put up with it. The point is, I reckon Pete Watson knows you an' him was plottin' somethin' together an' I reckon they've got him wherever they're holed up. No, sir, I don't give much for Sam's chances.'

'They're in the caves at the start of Payute Canyon,' said Jethro. 'Maybe you ought to get a posse together and set him free.'

'Son,' smiled Wally. 'You've been readin' too many of them dime novels or whatever they call 'em that I hear are all the rage back East. Things don't happen quite like that. First of all there's got to have been some sort of crime committed and secondly a sheriff can't form a posse just like that. All he can do is ask for volunteers, but if nobody wants to join, he can't force 'em, an' I can assure you there ain't one person in the whole of Henderson who gives a damn what happens to Sam Chisholm.'

'I do,' said Jethro, remembering the words of the minister when he blamed himself for the deaths of others due to his own inaction. He had persuaded Scruffy to ride out that morning and whatever had happened was largely due to him.

'Then I guess you're the feller to do somethin' about it if you're that bothered,' smiled Wally.

SIX

The more Jethro thought about it, the more concerned he became and the feeling that he had condemned Scruffy to death would not go away. It was obvious that Wally Hutchinson was not going to be of any help so he went to talk to the Reverend James Gough, although he had the feeling that he, too, would not be very helpful and in truth he did not know what the minister would be able to do.

'Unfortunately, Wally is right,' said the minister, confirming his suspicions. 'Sam Chisholm has been around for as long as anyone can remember but I don't know anyone who has a good word to say for him or who would be prepared to help him, at least not unless by helping him they were helping themselves, but that applies to a great many things, not just Sam Chisholm.'

'Does that include you?' asked Jethro.

'To be perfectly honest,' nodded the minister, 'I suppose it must. From a purely selfish point of view, Sam Chisholm has never done anything for the church and, as far as I am aware, he has never so much as set foot inside one. In fact, he has often said that he considers churches and churchmen to be parasites on the rest of society. He should talk about being a parasite!'

'Is he?' said Jethro, somehow feeling that someone had to defend Scruffy. 'How is he a parasite? From what I hear he pays his way by one means or another. I know he tries sponging drinks in the saloon, but I expect there's a great many others who do the same. He doesn't strike me as better or worse than anyone else and I can't understand this total indifference as to whether he gets murdered or not. Whatever he is or whatever he does, he's still a human being and deserves to be treated as such just as long as he does-n't cause anyone any trouble or harm.'

'Here endeth the first lesson!' smiled the minister. 'You are quite right, son, I should not be condemn-ing any man just because he doesn't share my beliefs or does not live quite the same as I do. I don't think it's going to do you much good trying to get Wally to act though. I am sorry to say this, but if you feel so strongly about what happens to him, you are the only person who can deal with it.'

'I could be too late,' said Jethro, having made up his mind, 'but at least I'm going out there to see if there is anything I can do, especially since I got him into it in the first place.'

'I knew it!' grated Humpback Chisholm. 'You was lyin' through the stumps of your teeth. You was seen talkin' to the young feller in the saloon on Saturday night.'

'I was tryin' to bum a drink,' protested Scruffy. 'You know me, I'll try bummin' drinks off anyone. I didn't actually talk to him, honest I didn't.'

'That's not what we heard,' said Ernie Price. 'We heard he bought you quite a few drinks. That don't sound like not talkin'.'

'Yeh,' grated Humpback. 'You was tryin' to get him to kill us just 'cos you is shit scared to do it yourself. I know you've tried it on with other folk what have been passin' through, but this is the first time anyone's taken you up on it.'

'Mind you,' said Pete Watson, 'he is the first one who has had cause. It's our own fault, I guess, we should've made sure he was dead.'

'That ain't no excuse!' snapped Humpback. 'He might be my brother and sure, I suppose I did murder his wife an' daughter, but I was blind drunk at the time an' didn't know what I was doin'. They told me I raped both of 'em first, but I sure don't remember doin' that. Maybe I did an' maybe I didn't. The thing is I can understand why he should hate my guts an' want to see me dead, but he just ain't got the nerve to do it himself.' He tossed his revolver towards his brother. 'Go ahead, Sam, pick it up. It's loaded, all you have to do is point it an' shoot.' Scruffy licked his lips and moved away from the gun as though it were some deadly snake about to strike. 'See,' laughed Humpback. 'Shit scared!' He picked up the gun and pressed it to Scruffy's temple and pulled back the hammer. 'Bang! You're dead!' he laughed. He eased the hammer down and replaced the gun in its holster. 'That would be too easy, Sam, much too easy.'

'The whole point is,' said Clubfoot Higgins, 'because of what he did, Curly is dead. He might as well have killed him himself, but I agree with Humpy, he wouldn't have the guts to do anythin' like that, it must've been this Jethro Smith feller.'

'Hangin' is the penalty for murder,' said Ernie
Price. 'I say we hang him.' Scruffy gulped and automatically rubbed his hand around his neck.

'How say you, gentlemen of the jury?' said Pete
Watson, standing in front of them and catching his
thumbs under the lapel of his jacket and puffing his
chest out. 'Do you find the defendant guilty or not
guilty of the murder of one James Henry Johnson,
otherwise known as Curly because he was completely
bald?'

'Guilty!' came the combined response.

'As guilty as if he had squeezed the trigger
himself,' added Humpback. He, too, stood up and
faced the others and gripped the collar of his shirt. 'I
suppose that as the only living relative of the accused,
I ought to submit a plea for mercy – I ought to but I
don't see why the hell I should.' They all laughed.

'Sam Chisholm,' intoned Pete Watson, 'you have
been tried and found guilty of the murder of Curly
Johnson. It is the decision of this court that you be
taken from this place and hanged by the neck until
you are dead.' They all laughed and cheered. 'There
is just one minor problem,' continued Pete. 'The
nearest tree is about five miles away.'

'There's that old, dead thorn tree up on the
ridge,' said Ernie. 'It ain't a tall tree but it should be
high enough to take a rope an' him.'

'The old thorn tree!' agreed everyone.

'Come on, Sam, up on that mule of yours,' said
Humpback. 'We is goin' to have us a hangin'!'

Although there was no way of knowing what, if
anything, had happened to Scruffy Chisholm, Jethro

knew that he had to act quickly if he was to stand any real chance of saving him. Like Wally Hutchinson and the minister, he was convinced that even Scruffy's own brother, Humpback, would have no hesitation in killing him if what he had learned and had been told by Scruffy himself were even half true. The fact that he felt the need to act was one thing, actually taking that action was another. Payute Flats was just that – flat – and from what Jethro remembered, getting anywhere near the caves without being seen was almost impossible. However, this did not dampen his determination and he rode out of Henderson half an hour after talking to the minister knowing that he would just have to take his chances as they arrived.

Jethro estimated that the five riders were about half a mile away, although he knew that on the seemingly endless flats, distances could be very deceptive. At first he deliberately kept out of sight in one of the many gullies as he watched their progress towards what appeared to be the only tree for miles and that had a distinctly dead appearance. He was quite certain that these were the four remaining murderers of his family and that the fifth man was Scruffy Chisholm, if only from the fact that he was the only one riding a mule.

Keeping himself out of sight proved something of a problem since he had to regularly come out of the gully to check on their progress, but now reasonably certain that their general direction was towards the dead tree, which was between himself and them, he tethered his horse to a dry bush in a hollow and made his way forward on foot, rifle and revolver at the ready, still with no idea just what he was going to do. The thought suddenly struck him that it was equally possible that Scruffy was a willing traveller, although if what he had told him was true, that possibility seemed rather unlikely.

The group reached the tree whilst Jethro was still about 200 yards away and, although he did manage to get closer, he was in no position to take any action. A shot from his rifle might carry as far as the tree, but its accuracy would be anything but reliable, besides which, at that moment, since they appeared to have dismounted, he was unable to distinguish Scruffy from the others, so any shot might hit the man he was trying to save.

Eventually, after a lot of activity around the tree, the mule was pulled into position beneath it and Scruffy forced, plainly protesting and struggling, on to its back, apparently with his hands tied behind him. It suddenly dawned on Jethro what was about to happen. Not caring too much if he would be seen or not, Jethro ran along a gully in order to get himself closer. When he judged that he was about as close as he could possibly get, he clambered up the gully and stood in full view. His rifle was at his shoulder and being fired in almost the same instant that the mule was whipped forward and Scruffy was snatched off its back, his feet kicking and jerking as he swung by his neck on the rope.

Whether the bullet from Jethro's rifle hit one of them, he did not know and did not really care, although none of them reacted as though they had been hit as they leapt on their horses. A couple of shots were sent in Jethro's general direction, but they fell well short and the men did not appear very keen on standing their ground and making a fight of it. They rode off at speed down the ridge and were soon lost in a cloud of dust.

Immediately the men had ridden off, Jethro was racing towards the tree and the body still jerking on the end of the rope, yelling at Scruffy to keep still, but it seemed that his calls went unheard as Scruffy continued to kick and struggle. Fortunately Jethro always carried a knife and when he reached Scruffy, he grabbed hold of his body to steady it while he reached up and managed to cut through the rope allowing them to crash to the ground just as Scruffy's struggles were beginning to weaken, but from the rasping and gasping noises coming from the now almost purple features, it was obvious that Scruffy was still very much alive. Jethro loosened the rope around his neck and cut through the rope on his wrists. Scruffy eventually managed to regain some sort of control of himself and suddenly stared into Jethro's face, plainly not believing what he was seeing.

'I'll say this for you, son,' he gasped, tugging at the rope around his neck, 'you sure are a sight for sore eyes, but you gotta do somethin' about your timin', you did leave it a bit late.'

'You've just got to be thankful I was able to get out here at all,' grinned Jethro, standing up and scanning the flats. 'The pity is that I didn't get chance to kill one of them.'

'I wouldn't concern yourself too much about that,' gulped Scruffy, removing the remains of the rope and rubbing his hand round his neck, which was bleeding slightly as a result of the rope burns. 'They sure as hell know just who you are an' after what you've just done to 'em, killin' Curly an' now settin' me free, I'd say you were number one on their list of folk to kill an' believe me, they enjoy doin' just that.'

Jethro examined the marks on Scruffy's neck and, although there did not appear to be any permanent damage, he thought that Doc Galloway had better be consulted. Scruffy on the other hand was not entirely convinced that Doc Galloway was the best person.

'If anyone's got to take a look, I'd prefer it to be Hal Morgan.'

'Hal Morgan?' queried Jethro.

'Yeh,' nodded Scruffy. 'He's the veterinarian an' at least he ain't a drunkard like Doc Galloway. He's better'n the doc when it comes to pullin' teeth an' settin' broken bones as well.'

'Well I think it had better be Doc Galloway,' asserted Jethro. 'Especially as I shall probably have to pay the bill. So what was all that about?' Scruffy explained what had happened as they rode back to Henderson.

'So are you layin' any complaints?' Wally Hutchinson demanded harshly of Scruffy. 'I don't care who saw what, if you don't lay a complaint I can't do nothin'.' From his manner it was plain that he did not want anything to do with Sam Chisholm or his problems, an attitude which surprised Jethro since he had formed the opinion that Wally Hutchinson was a very fair-minded sheriff even though he had made his feelings plain earlier. 'Then, of course, there's the question of catchin' them,' continued Wally. 'They could be chased around them hills and plains for years an' never get caught, usin' the border to avoid everyone. That's just what they've been doin' all this time.

'I get the message, Wally!' grunted Scruffy. 'OK, forget all about it. If it had been left to me I wouldn't have bothered you at all, but this young feller thought he knew best, it was his idea to tell you.' He turned to Jethro and smiled sardonically. 'See, son, just like I said, nobody wants to know anythin' about folk like me. We is too much trouble. I reckon he'd've been only too pleased if I had been hanged.'

'That's what it seems like,' agreed Jethro, looking hard at Wally. 'I had you down for a good and fair lawman, but it looks like I was wrong.'

'It ain't a case of not bein' interested,' sighed Wally, 'I'm just bein' practical. OK, Jethro, Sam has a good case on the face of it. Doc Galloway can confirm that there were rope marks round his neck and you can swear that you saw them try to hang him and that you had to cut him off the tree. That's fine, but like I said, it could take a long time to catch them. I know they were in town this mornin', but that's the first time they've been anywhere near Henderson in almost six months. You've got title to land which is the best part of another five or six hundred miles from here and unless you're prepared to hang about waitin' for the day they do ride into town an' I can arrest 'em, I lose the main witness an' we end up just where we've allus ended up, not bein' able to prove a damned thing against 'em. Believe me, I would act if I could an' if there was anythin' like a good chance they'd be convicted.'

'So why can't you go after them?' asked Jethro.

'Sure, I could do that,' nodded Wally, 'but the chances of me gettin' back here alive are almost nil, let alone bringin' them in. I don't know whether you noticed or not, son, but on your way over from the East it must've dawned on you that there's an awful lot of land out here, land in which a man could lose himself forever if he wanted to. Some of the bleakest of that land is right here around Henderson.

'Don't ask me about a posse either; I told you before, folk just wouldn't want to take the risk, not for a Chisholm. Their mother was more trouble than she was worth an' most folk wanted her runnin' out of town.'

'See what I meant, son?' grinned Scruffy. 'Don't you worry your head about it, if you've got land to go to, you just go on right ahead an' let Wally here worry about me gettin' murdered by my own brother.'

'I don't intend leaving this town until those four men are either dead or they've been arrested for what they did to my folk, and since it appears that they can't be arrested, although I can't see for the life of me why not since I don't know what other proof you need, I suppose I shall just have to kill them and risk the consequences.'

'Just so long as anythin' you do is legal, in self-defence or is out of my territory I don't much care what you do,' said Wally.

Both Jethro and Scruffy shrugged, left the sheriff and headed for the saloon where Jethro paid for all they drank. Jimmy did tell them of the visit he had had from the gang, although he, too, did not appear to have any interest in what happened to Scruffy.

'So what do you think they'll do next?' Jethro asked, as he and Scruffy took their drinks to a corner table. 'You know them better than most folk, you must have some idea.'

'I'll have to think about that,' slurped Scruffy, through his beer. 'I don't know 'em all that well, even if one of 'em is my twin brother. The one thing I am sure of is that they'll be after the pair of us from here on in, probably you more'n me.'

'So what do I do?' sighed Jethro.

'If I was in your boots, son,' slurped Scruffy again. 'I'd get me out of here just as fast as I could an' to hell with what happens to anyone else. Believe me, that's just what I'd do.' He looked up at Jethro and smiled. 'I know you think Wally an' the minister are good folk, but you'd better believe even they wouldn't lose no sleep if'n you was to go an' get yourself killed.'

'Yeh!' Jethro sighed again, nodding his head. 'You are probably right at that. The fact is those men killed my parents and my sister and they raped both my sister and my mother. For their sakes I just can't ride out and not do anything about it. You must have felt the same about your wife and daughter.'

'Sure did,' nodded Scruffy, sagely. 'An' I feel just the same now as I did then. Flora was the only woman what ever treated me like a normal man. To her it didn't seem to matter how I looked. She warn't no great looker herself, but at least she treated me real good. If I was younger I reckon I could deal with it myself, but I ain't. You've got the advantage over me, son. . . .' He raised his twisted hands and flexed his fingers. 'I got me these useless things to deal with apart from which I'm an old man now.'

'How old is old?' asked Jethro.

'Old enough to be no threat to nobody,' sighed Scruffy. 'I don't rightly know just how old me an Humpy are, 'cept that I'm older'n him by about half an hour. I feel kinda guilty in makin' use of you, son, but I hope you understand why.'

'I guess I'm just as guilty of making use of you,' smiled Jethro. 'If I hadn't they probably wouldn't have tried to hang you.'

'I guess somethin' like that had to happen some-time or another,' shrugged Scruffy. 'I'm just glad that it happened while you was around. Still, like I said, I reckon the best thing you could do is ride on out of Henderson an' forget all about me, 'specially since you got some land to go to.'

'The land can wait a while longer,' said Jethro.

'I have the feeling that something is about to happen,' said the Reverend James Gough. 'In fact, I have had the feeling ever since you rode into town with your wagon. We have rubbed along with Pete Watson and his gang for years, everyone complaining that something ought to be done about them but nobody daring to take it upon themselves to do anything and Wally not being able to act.'

'I would have thought there were times when they could have been arrested,' said Jethro. 'Apart from them coming into town and half the town being witness to them killing someone, what more proof does the sheriff need?'

'It's been tried,' smiled the minister. 'The trouble is we have a lawyer in town who really knows his stuff and twice he has got them off charges which every-one else was convinced would ensure their convic-tion. It's not that Mark Evans, the lawyer, is on their side, all he does is his job I suppose, and there's been more than one who has been grateful to him for doing just that. I guess you can't have everything going just the way you want it to all the time.'

'I can see what you mean,' sighed Jethro. 'That doesn't make it any the easier to accept though; I know what I saw and heard when my folks were murdered.'

The minister sighed and placed his hands together and thought for a few moments. Eventually he looked up at Jethro and smiled weakly. 'Both the wife and I know exactly how you feel and we are both hoping that you will succeed.' He sighed again and looked upwards. 'See, even ministers of religion are mere mortals, subject to all the feelings and emotions of other men. Outwardly I should be urging you to just accept what happened as the will of God, but we both know that that would be asking too much. I don't know what else I can say or do. Being in the position I am, there is not that much I can do. I certainly can't go with you to kill them, much as my feelings might want me to. Have you thought about what to do next?'

'It seems that I am now at the top of their list to be killed,' said Jethro after a few moments. 'If that is the case I suppose the logical thing for me to do would be to let them come to me, but I don't know how long that would take. I could ride out to them, but you must know what it's like out on Payute Flats, I'd be seen long before I could get close enough. The trouble with waiting for them to come to me is that I do have some land to claim and, according to the documents I have, I have to claim it within a year of the date on the certificate. That gives me another three months at the outside.'

'You could claim it and then come back,' said the minister.

'No,' said Jethro, shaking his head. 'That'd be too late, the moment would have passed and I'd never forgive myself for not acting before.'

'I know exactly what you mean,' smiled the minister. 'I let the moment pass once and I deeply regretted it for more than one reason.'

'Anyway,' sighed Jethro, 'there's nothing I can do today. I'll sleep on it and hope that something turns up in the next day or so.'

'Like I said,' smiled the minister, 'I have this feeling that something will turn up. I hope for all our sakes that it happens soon and Henderson can become a normal town again.'

SEVEN

Jethro slept well that night even though the problem of what to do about Pete Watson and his gang had occupied his thoughts all evening. He did not see Scruffy Chisholm at all and, in a way, was rather thankful. The first rays of dawn found him sitting on the front of his wagon trying to make up his mind whether or not to ride out to the caves at Payute Canyon in the hope that he would be early enough to surprise them, but he eventually decided that that approach simply would not work. Feeling hungry he went along to Grace Stallard's diner only to discover that the menu for breakfast was exactly the same as the menu for any other time of day – beef stew and dumplings or beef mince – he opted for the beef mince as being rather more digestible and palatable at that time of day, although when faced with it he found that he was not quite as hungry as he had thought. Nevertheless, he forced himself to eat on the basis that he had to eat something, but he decided that from that point onwards he would do his own cooking, at least it certainly could not be any worse than Grace Stallard's.

Scruffy Chisholm turned up about an hour after Jethro had eaten and suggested that the best thing to be done was to wait and see what would happen. He seemed quite certain that the gang would come looking for Jethro in the very near future. In the meantime, Scruffy announced, he was going looking for strays in the opposite direction to Payute Flats. The significance of this did not hit Jethro until after Scruffy had left.

For the next two hours, the people of Henderson went about their normal business and the sound of sawing and machinery could be heard from the mill as huge tree trunks were sawn up into planks. Sheriff Wally Hutchinson acknowledged him as he went past but made no attempt to talk. Jethro toyed with the idea of going to see the Reverend James Gough, but saw him and his wife leave town riding a buggy and assumed that they were going to visit one of their parishioners. Henderson was, to all outward appearances, much the same as any other small town almost anywhere in the country.

Normality was disrupted when a lone rider, on what was obviously a lumbering draught horse, came into town and immediately ran into the sheriff's office. Both he and Wally Hutchinson emerged a few moments later, Wally quickly saddling his horse, and both men riding off as fast as the draught horse could travel. Whilst he did wonder what was happening, Jethro did not really give the incident that much thought at the time.

The real disruption to normality occurred about ten minutes after Wally and the lone rider had left town and took the form of men suddenly running off the street and women gathering stray offspring and

joining their menfolk. Although he could see something of what was going on in the town from his
wagon, Jethro could not see everything and curiosity
eventually got the better of him. He tackled a woman
who was urging her children along the street to find
out exactly what was happening.

'Watson and Higgins!' gasped the woman.
'They've just come into town and gone into the
saloon.'

'So why the panic?' asked Jethro.

'Whenever any of that gang come in,' she panted,
gathering up the smallest child, 'it means trouble
and the sheriff isn't here to do anything about it.'
Jethro was about to ask her if it was only the two –
Watson and Higgins – but she did not wait around
long enough. By that time the streets of Henderson
were totally deserted and the only sounds to be heard
came from the sawmill and two barking dogs.

'Two of us should be able to deal with him,' said Pete
Watson, 'but we've got to get Wally Hutchinson out
of town somehow.'

'A fire!' suggested Ernie Price. 'A fire on one of
the outlyin' farms ought to get him out. We could
burn either the crops or the homestead or somethin'.'

'There's not all that much in the way of crops to
burn at this time of year,' said Pete Watson. 'We'll
have to burn the buildin's but not the homestead if
you can help it, maybe a barn or somethin'. Humpy,
you like playin' with fire, you an' Ernie go set light to
a farm. I reckon the Jones place out along Navaho
Creek would be about the best one.'

'Never did like that Jones feller either,' grinned

Humpback. 'Suits me fine. Don't you go killin' that no-good brother of mine though, he's mine an' it won't hurt him to sweat a bit.'

'That's it then,' said Pete. 'You an' Ernie go set the fire an' me an' Clubfoot go an' kill this Jethro Smith, after we're quite certain that the sheriff has left town.'

The four of them rode out together, Humpback and Ernie following the Navaho River and after about half an hour, Pete Watson and Clubfoot Higgins rode on to take up a position overlooking Henderson from where, some two hours later, they saw Jones and the sheriff ride out towards Navaho Creek.

Acting without really thinking, Jethro fastened his gunbelt and then practised a few fast draws, eventually satisfied that his recently acquired skills had not diminished. There was one thought in his mind – revenge. The question of legality and the possibility of being charged with murder did not form part of his thinking at that moment, all that mattered was the two men who were now in the saloon, one of whom was the leader of the gang that had murdered his parents and his sister giving his actions an added impulse.

The main street of Henderson was completely deserted, something which had probably never occurred before during normal daylight hours in the entire history of the town. The street itself may have been deserted but Jethro was very conscious of countless eyes peering from darkened rooms or through slits in draped windows watching his every step. He wondered just what those onlookers expected and whether it really mattered to them what happened to him or to Watson and Higgins. He doubted very much if any tears would be shed whomsoever it was Sam Trickett, the undertaker, placed in one of his boxes. The most likely thing to happen, should he be fortunate enough to dispose of Watson and Higgins, was that he would enjoy a temporary few moments of glory as he was lauded by the citizens of Henderson.

That was the point: should he be fortunate enough. For the first time he realized exactly what he was about to do and its full implication. There were two of them and he had no doubt that they had ridden into town with one particular aim – to kill him. As good as he might be with a gun, he had no way of judging exactly how good he would be against experienced men like Watson and Higgins, other than assurances from the Reverend James Gough that he was good enough. The thought also struck him that Wally Hutchinson's sudden departure from Henderson had been very convenient for the two men in the saloon and he somehow knew that the sheriff's departure had been arranged. For a very brief moment, his steps along the centre of the main street faltered and the thought flashed across his mind that he ought to turn back. He straightened himself and strode on, banishing all such thoughts from his mind.

In a way, it came as something of a surprise that Jethro found himself standing in the centre of the street staring hard at the swing doors of the saloon, a strange dryness in his mouth and throat, his hand resting on the handle of his gun, ready to draw and shoot should anyone suddenly burst through those

swing doors. Time meant nothing as he stood and
watched and he really did not have any idea if it was
a matter of seconds or minutes, but, eventually, as it
became obvious that the two men were not about to
come out to him, he decided that it was up to him to
go inside to them.

As he stepped up on to the boardwalk, it seemed
that the distant hum of the sawmill chose that precise
moment to stop, as did the singing of the few small
birds and even the sound of the wind. For a few
moments it appeared that the world itself had
stopped and the only sounds were from Jethro's
boots as he crossed the boardwalk. It seemed that
everyone and everything was waiting expectantly as
he pushed against the swing doors. . . .

As Jethro had expected, there were only three
people in the saloon, Jimmy the bartender, Clubfoot
Higgins and Pete Watson. Of the three, only Jimmy
bothered to look at him and he seemed to know
better than to ask Jethro if he wanted a drink and
Jethro did not ask for one as he crossed the wooden
floor, his footsteps echoing eerily around the almost
empty room. The two men still did not turn to look
at him, although he was well aware that they were
studying his reflection closely in the large mirror
behind the bar. There were a few moments of
complete silence before the two men slowly turned
to face Jethro and then there followed a further few
moments of silent challenge between them.

'I guess you heard we was in town,' sneered Pete
Watson. 'I had a bet with Clubfoot here that you
wouldn't show up. It's one bet I don't mind losin'.'

'I heard,' confirmed Jethro. 'Sorry I had to spoil your little party with Sam Chisholm.'

'Yeh,' sneered Clubfoot, 'He always was the lucky one. All that's about to change though. First you an' then Sam.'

'Killing me will probably mean you being charged with murder,' Jethro pointed out. Both men laughed and straightened themselves.

'We got us a very good witness who will say that you died in a fair fight,' grinned Watson. He looked at Jimmy who had chosen that moment to polish some glasses for at least the third time. 'Ain't that right, Jimmy, you can swear that we killed him in self-defence?' Jimmy did not look up or react in any way except to rub harder at the glass in his hand. 'See,' gloated Watson, 'a witness nobody could find fault with.'

'Only because he knows you would kill him if he said anything else,' said Jethro. 'You don't think Wally Hutchinson would be fooled do you?'

'It don't matter much what that idiot thinks,' laughed Clubfoot, 'it's what the court thinks what counts an' I can't see no jury in these parts findin' us guilty. Besides, Mark Evans, the lawyer, is a real stickler for facts; he's got us off more'n one charge before now.'

'OK,' sighed Jethro, beginning to tire of what had turned into something of a cat-and-mouse situation. 'Go ahead and shoot.' This actually had the effect of making Watson and Higgins glance uneasily at each other. It was apparently not something they had expected and it appeared to catch them off guard. They moved slowly into the centre of the room, placing themselves between Jethro and the door. 'I'm waiting!' sneered Jethro, perhaps with a premature feeling that he had somehow acquired the upper hand.

Watson and Higgins once again glanced a little nervously at each other; this was a new experience as they were accustomed to everyone being frightened of them and this seemingly arrogant youth was very much an unknown quantity. Like all of their type, they did not really appreciate being faced with the unknown and untested.

Jethro waited, determined that he was not going to be the one to make the first move despite the fact that he fully intended, if possible, to kill both men. It was partly this stance by Jethro which made the two men feel rather apprehensive. Once again Pete Watson and Clubfoot Higgins glanced nervously at each other. Suddenly both men moved. . . .

Jethro thought that he had only fired two shots, although when he checked his gun later he discovered that three chambers had been used. How many shots had been fired by Watson and Higgins he never discovered; all he knew was that one of their bullets had shattered into his arm and that at least one of his had found its mark – Clubfoot Higgins lay on the floor with blood oozing from a hole in his chest.

What had happened to Pete Watson he did not know at the time. He did not actually see him run from the saloon, but that was what he had apparently done the instant he saw his companion fall. Ignoring the pain in his arm, Jethro examined the body of Clubfoot Higgins and smiled with satisfaction when he discovered that he was dead.

'Two down, three to go!' he heard himself saying,

looking up to discover that the previously empty saloon had suddenly become quite full as at least ten men gathered round, all except one having come in through the back door the moment Pete Watson had mounted his horse and fled town. One of them was quite adamant that Watson had been injured, although nobody else could confirm this.

Doc Galloway was called to examine Jethro and to confirm that Clubfoot Higgins was in fact dead. The bullet had apparently passed through Jethro's arm, leaving a clean wound into which Doc Galloway poured some of his cure-all tincture. He then bound it tightly, with instructions to Jethro that he was to see him the next day and have the wound checked.

Almost an hour later, Wally Hutchinson returned and did not appear at all surprised when told what had happened. He questioned Jimmy briefly and appeared satisfied that it had been a fair fight, at least as far as Jethro was concerned.

'The fire out at the Jones farm had been started deliberately,' he told both Jimmy and Jethro. 'Fortunately, it didn't do too much damage, just some hay and the barn itself, but the folk round here will all turn out to help build a new one an' give some of their own hay. A barn buildin' is always a good excuse for a get-together an' a barn dance. I got back here as quick as I could, but I had to stay awhile and help out an' look for evidence.'

'So what are you going to do about Pete Watson and the others?' asked Jethro.

'Nothin'!' replied Wally, very firmly.

'Nothing?' gaped Jethro. 'What more proof do you need? It's obvious that they arranged the fire and then rode into town intending to kill me.'

'What proof?' laughed Wally. 'Mark Evans would be able to tear any charge to pieces in no time. Two men – OK, maybe they ain't the nicest of characters – come into town simply to have a drink; there ain't no law against that. Some young hothead who is quite convinced that they killed his folk challenges them. Fortunately for the hothead, he comes off better than they do. One of them is killed – although there is a reliable witness to say it was a fair fight – and the other gets out of town as fast as he can. That'd be understandable, he's scared he's goin' to be killed as well. So far there isn't a damn thing I could charge 'em with that Mark Evans couldn't get them off, so it just ain't worth the bother. Don't get me wrong, son, we all know what they intended to do, it's just that there ain't sufficient proof.'

'It seems to me that this lawyer, Mark Evans, must be on their side,' objected Jethro. 'Everything seems to revolve on what he might or might not do.'

'Now that's just where you're wrong,' said Wally. 'Mark Evans is probably the finest and certainly the fairest lawyer in the territory. You just provide him with one shred of real evidence, evidence that will stand up in court, and he'll be the first to go along with it.'

'In the meantime, there's nothing anyone can do and they are free to come and go as they please,' objected Jethro. 'Can't anything be done?'

'Seems to me you're doin' a pretty good job single-handed,' grinned Jimmy, as he polished yet another glass for about the tenth time. 'You said yourself, two down, three to go. You handled yourself pretty damn good just now; they didn't expect you to be that good and, frankly, neither did I. As you say, that's two down, the only trouble is the next three might not be quite so easy, they now know just what to expect and they won't be taken by surprise again.'

The Reverend James and Mrs Gough appeared genuinely sorry that they had not been in town to witness the incident, but both had been called to one of the outlying farms to administer to the needs of an old man who was on the verge of death. In fact he had died whilst they had been there. However, the reverend was still of the opinion that Jethro was in need of yet more practice and took the young man out to Navaho Creek where he spent the remainder of that day and part of the following day forcing Jethro to repeat various movements time and time again. In the end, Jethro was quite convinced that he could have performed them in his sleep if the need ever arose. The only new thing he learned was to handle his rifle in such a way that it almost became an extension of his arm.

That evening, Jethro was the talk of Henderson as most of the male population crowded into the saloon to stare in awe at the spot where Clubfoot Higgins had met his demise. They all stood respectfully to one side as Jethro entered, this time minus his guns, and it seemed that nobody dared even talk to the great man. Jethro ordered a beer – for which Jimmy refused payment saying that it was due to him that he was having one of the best nights he had had in a long time. Apart from a few casual remarks, everyone avoided Jethro apart from a very well-dressed man, perhaps ten years older than Jethro, who stood alongside him, ordered a large whiskey – which was very noticeably served from a bottle under the

counter and not from behind the bar – who then
suggested to Jethro that they occupy an empty table
in the far corner of the room.

'Mark Evans,' announced the man, extending his
hand to Jethro who took it and shook it briefly.
'Perhaps you have heard of me,' he went on.

'Sure, I've heard of you,' nodded Jethro sitting
opposite the lawyer. 'It seems to me that it's really
you who runs this town and not the sheriff.'

'Nor the mayor,' grinned Evans. 'I get accused of
having them all in my pocket every now and then.'

'You're younger than I expected,' said Jethro. 'I
had imagined a much older man. You're the feller
who won't let Wally arrest Pete Watson and his men.'

'Wrong!' smiled Evans. 'It is entirely up to Wally
who he arrests and for what. All I can do is ensure
that whomsoever he does arrest is held on a charge
which is safe and legal.'

'Seems to me that's just about the same thing,'
said Jethro.

'I can understand how you must feel,' said the
lawyer. 'Personally I have little doubt that those men
are the ones who murdered your family and I know
exactly how you feel about the law's seeming impo-
tence and my own apparent intransigence, but it is
hard enough trying to instil a sense of right and
wrong out in these parts as it is, which is why I try to
enforce a very strict interpretation of the law. My
hope is that my persistence will pay off and that one
day we will have a legal system we can rely on and be
proud of. Coming from the East you must be aware
of the difference.'

'Can't say that I ever really thought about it,'
admitted Jethro. 'I always accepted that that was the

way things were back East. The point is, I know those men murdered my family and I shan't rest until they have been punished for it and, since it appears that the law is about as effective as fart, all wind and no substance, I have to do it myself.'

'That, unfortunately, is the kind of attitude I am fighting against,' sighed the lawyer. He held his hand up to silence Jethro who was about to object. 'Please, believe me when I say that I do not blame you in the least. I must confess that this territory and my task would be that much better and easier for not having men like Pete Watson about. In the meantime, I simply do my best to ensure fairness for all.'

'But you wouldn't hesitate in sending me to the gallows if I killed one of them in cold blood,' said Jethro.

'On the contrary,' smiled Evans, 'I would do my best to ensure that you were found not guilty. I am a defence lawyer, not a prosecuting lawyer, although most of my work is taken up with mundane work connected with land rights and disputes. Personally I wish you the best of luck in your crusade and I hope that you succeed. I just felt that it was about time I made myself known to you to correct certain misconceptions which I was certain you had.'

'Thanks,' said Jethro, looking at the lawyer in a new light. Evans drank his whiskey, nodded to Jethro who had the distinct impression that he had just been dismissed from a royal presence and he disappeared amongst the crowd. Almost immediately he was replaced by Scruffy Chisholm who, for a change, arrived carrying a glass of beer. Jethro did not dare ask him where he had got it, feeling reasonably certain that he had either bummed it, or there was someone who was at the moment looking round for a mislaid glass.

'I heard about Clubfoot,' whispered Scruffy confidentially, as though it was something as yet unknown by everyone else. 'You must be better'n I thought; old Clubfoot warn't no slouch when it came to handlin' a gun.'

'I guess I just got lucky,' nodded Jethro. 'I got me a bullet through my arm. Luckily it's my left arm. Pretty soon the whole thing will be shot away.'

'I believe in ridin' luck while it's with you,' grinned Scruffy. 'You killed two of 'em, it shouldn't take that long to finish off the others.'

'What you mean is you believe in riding my luck,' said Jethro. 'I know they have you marked down as a dead man and since you don't seem capable of dealing with them yourself, you need me to do it for you.'

'Give me a new pair of hands an' I'll show you just how much help I need,' sneered Scruffy, holding up his twisted, gnarled, misshapen hands. 'OK, son, I admit I'm makin' use of you, but I can help too. There ain't nobody knows this territory better'n I do; I could find what they call the needle in the haystack out there if I had to. Right now, the other three will have gone to ground an' only I know where they're like as not to be. If they ain't there I'll find 'em; I can follow a fish through water if needs be.'

Jethro sighed and took a drink of his beer. 'I must admit that nothing would please me better than to get all this sorted out and be on my way. I've got me some land to lay claim to.'

'Then you just listen to the ramblin's of an old man,' grinned Scruffy. 'Wally Hutchinson could search out there for the rest of his life an' never find 'em. Stick with me an' I guarantee that you'll have them within two days.'

'Or guarantee that I'll be dead,' smiled Jethro.

'In which case you won't have no more problems!' grinned Scruffy.

EIGHT

Scruffy Chisholm and Jethro left Henderson just as the first rays of sunlight were beginning to show on the distant horizon and even at that early hour, the shop and store owners were in the process of removing their shutters in preparation for another day's business. Jethro would have liked to have travelled much faster, but he was in the hands of a man to whom time really meant very little and who rode only a mule – a very stubborn and slow mule it transpired. He resigned himself to a long, slow journey across baking hot plains and it was not very long before he was beginning to rue not having taken a larger water canteen, or even two, although it appeared that even Scruffy, who had great experience of Payute Flats, only had one medium-size canteen. When he had agreed to the venture, Jethro had not really given much thought as to how long they would be away from Henderson or to what the temperature would be, although common sense ought to have told him that it would be extremely hot, especially around midday. As he talked to Scruffy, it appeared that the old man expected them to be out at least one night, possibly even longer and when questioned about water, he simply shrugged and laughed. All Jethro could hope for now was that Scruffy knew where there was water and that he had had the foresight to bring some food, something else that Jethro had not even considered. All-in-all, Jethro realized that he had a lot to learn about survival in the arid and inhospitable lands of the West.

For the first two hours conditions were not too bad, the morning breeze was cool and there were just enough clouds in the sky to keep off the worst effects of the sun. However, once they had started across Payute Flats, the cloud suddenly disappeared and the temperature of the breeze increased quite a few degrees and offered little relief from the relentless sun, added to which the still relatively low position of the sun reflected off the salty flats making it very difficult to see any distance. It was only after they had been out of Henderson about three hours that Jethro realized that they were not heading towards the caves at Payute Canyon.

'Thought we'd try up at Puma Rocks first,' said Scruffy, when questioned about the change of direction. 'After what happened I don't reckon they'll be out at the caves, they wouldn't want to chance Wally goin' out after 'em.'

'And are they likely to be at this Puma Rocks place?' asked Jethro.

'Could be they is, could be they ain't,' shrugged Scruffy with a laugh. 'If they is we'll've saved a lot of time.'

'And if they're not?' prompted Jethro.

'Then we got us some other places to look,'

replied Scruffy casually. Jethro sighed and resigned himself to finding nothing.

An hour later, Scruffy pointed at some rocks about a quarter of a mile away and announced that these were Puma Rocks. Even Jethro could see how the rocks had acquired their name; from the angle they were approaching they did indeed give the appearance of a huge, crouching mountain lion. At the same time as he pointed out the rocks, Scruffy turned his mule down into one of the many gullies saying that it was time to get out of sight. Jethro was actually of the opinion that had anyone been watching from Puma Rocks they would have witnessed their approach long before this. When he made this observation known to Scruffy, the old man simply laughed and tapped the side of his nose knowingly, a habit which was beginning to annoy Jethro.

'Easy to see you ain't a plainsman,' he said. 'I'll take a wager with you when we get through all this, son. You get yourself atop them rocks an' see if you can see me comin'. I'll guarantee that you won't see me until I'm less than about two hundred yards away, if then. You wouldn't believe how difficult it is to pick out a man on a horse out here. A whole posse could get real close before anyone realized it was there.' Jethro found such a thing difficult to believe but he had to acknowledge that the old man probably knew what he was talking about.

The gully appeared to deepen as they approached the rocks and, after a time, in a particularly deep stretch in which there was a small pool of water, Scruffy indicated that they should dismount and make their way up the rocks on foot. They did not bother to tether the animals, Scruffy maintaining that neither would stray very far from the water and the sparse vegetation which surrounded it.

Gaining access to the rocks proved fairly easy as Scruffy led the way along yet another gully which, although shallower than the first, led directly into the base of the rocks. This time Scruffy placed a finger to his lips and waved Jethro into the shade of an overhang where both men listened intently.

'Don't think they is here,' Scruffy suddenly whispered. 'I'd've heard 'em by now if they had been. I'm goin' up to take a look. You can come with me if you want or you can stay here.' Jethro volunteered to accompany Scruffy, although he was very uncertain if it was a wise thing to do or not.

The central part of Puma Rocks proved to be almost a perfect circle of flat ground, perhaps a hundred feet across and completely surrounded by large rocks, giving the impression of a fortress. The only way in and out appeared to be by the way they had entered and it did not need any great intelligence to show that their quarry was not there. Jethro clambered up to the top of one of the surrounding rocks whilst Scruffy busied himself below, apparently looking for something, although Jethro had no idea nor any particular interest in what that something might be.

Although the rocks were not all that high, perhaps twenty feet, they gave a commanding view over much of Payute Flats. After staring at the flats for some time and discovering that his eyes very quickly became sore and watery, restricting his vision, Jethro was forced to concede that it would be very difficult to pick out anyone below. More than once he imagined that he could see men riding, but they just as suddenly seemed to evaporate and he dismissed such sightings. He was eventually joined by Scruffy who appeared rather smug and self-satisfied.

'They was here,' he announced. 'I reckon they must've left about two hours ago, maybe three, but no more. I found the embers of a fire still warm.'

'A fire out here?' queried Jethro.

'Sure,' grinned Scruff. 'There ain't no hotter place on earth durin' the day, but at night it can freeze you to the marrow. There's more'n one stranger found that out. I can take you to three skellingtons that've been out here a few years now.'

'Skeletons,' corrected Jethro, nodding. 'OK, so they were here. The question is where are they now? It seems to me they could either be miles away or just a few yards.'

'See!' said Scruffy, triumphantly, 'Didn't take you long to find out how easy it is to blend in. Where is they? We won't know that till we find 'em,' he said logically. 'What we got to do now is find their tracks an' follow 'em.'

Finding their tracks apparently proved a lot easier than Jethro had expected, although he had to admit that he would have been confused by what appeared to be conflicting signs. Scruffy, however, seemed to know exactly what he was looking at and had no doubts as to which direction they had taken. He pointed north.

'Stillwater Pass,' he said. 'There wouldn't be much point in goin' that direction unless they were headin' for Stillwater Pass. There ain't nothin' else for more'n two hundred miles, but that's the way they've gone right enough.' Jethro was still a little confused and not at all certain that the tracks they were following were even made by horses or any other creature. For the most part they appeared to be little more than wind-blown marks and most certainly could have been of any age, but he had to bow to Scruffy's obviously superior knowledge and expertise in such matters and at the same time vowed that he would have to learn the art of tracking.

'So why would they want to go to this Stillwater Pass?' he asked.

'Perfect place to hole up,' said Scruffy. 'Plenty of water, reasonable huntin' an' easy to either defend or keep out of sight if they want to.'

'OK, that's fine from their point of view,' said Jethro. 'If it's that easy to defend there doesn't seem a lot of point in us going there.'

Scruffy laughed and tapped the side of his nose again and wrinkled his weatherbeaten face even more. 'Trust me, son,' he said. 'I've been around these parts all my life an' I think I've learnt a thing or two in that time. Providin' you know what you is doin' an' you've got some kind of a head for heights, we can get up among 'em before they can see us.'

'How far?' sighed Jethro, now resigned to continuing a search about which he was beginning to have serious doubts.

'About five or six hours at the rate my old mule normally sees fit to go,' said Scruffy. 'Maybe seven or eight if she's feelin' a mite difficult. You could make it in about two or three hours on your own.'

Jethro was almost tempted to strike out on his own, but had enough sense to realize that he was, at that moment, dependent upon the old man. They returned to the gully and the pool of water where they had left their animals, refilled their canteens with what proved to be rather coloured and tepid water and continued their journey across the now even hotter salt flats, what breeze there was blowing into their faces making it difficult not to inhale the thirst-making salt even though both men had wrapped their kerchiefs around their faces and mouths.

The first signs of nightfall were beginning to descend on Payute Flats when Scruffy pointed ahead to two mountains which had been hitherto hidden by the heat-haze but suddenly appeared as the heat of the day subsided, announcing that they were within sight of Stillwater Pass. The journey had taken almost seven hours and they were still about an hour's ride away. The main reason for their very slow progress had been the extra stubbornness of Scruffy's mule and no amount of shouting, beating or cajoling had succeeded in making her go any faster.

From that point onwards, the previously hot, glaring saltiness of the flats gave way to sparse vegetation and it was something of a task to prevent either the mule or the horse from stopping to eat. Quite suddenly, however, both animals quickened their pace and appeared to head onwards with a new purpose.

'Water!' announced Scruffy. 'They can smell water. There's a pool up ahead, but I shouldn't think Pete Watson is there, too open.' Jethro strained his eyes ahead but could see nothing. 'I reckon I can smell it myself,' continued Scruffy. 'Just let 'em run, they know what they is doin'.'

It transpired that the animals did know where they

were going and about twenty minutes later mule and horse were greedily drinking while Jethro and Scruffy wallowed, fully clothed, in a large, deep pool of clear water set amongst a ring of rocks.

'I needed that,' said Jethro, as he staggered from the pool wiping his face. He glanced at the sun and realized that it was probably too late to consider moving on. 'I say we stay here the night,' he said.

'There ain't nothin' else we can do,' said Scruffy. 'It's about another hour to the mountain an' by the time we could reach more water it'd be way past sundown anyhow. We rest here the night an' start out at first light.'

'I'm hungry,' Jethro complained. 'I never even thought about bringing any food, what have you got?'

'The one thing you gotta learn out here is allus have somethin' to eat with you,' smiled Scruffy. 'That means you have to learn to like jerky, that's just about the only thing which don't go to rot in this heat. It tastes pretty revoltin', like eatin' your saddle, which in a way it is, leastways it's all made out of cow hide.' He produced a very dirty-looking cloth from his saddle-bag and unwrapped it. Almost immediately flies appeared from the previously lifeless desert and surrounded the dried meat. Scruffy did not even seem to notice them as he cut off a sizeable piece and handed it to Jethro. Jethro had great difficulty in keeping the flies at bay.

'Best way to eat jerky is to cut off a chunk small enough to swallow, chewin' it ain't no good,' continued Scruffy. 'The best that can be said about it is that it fills your stomach.' Jethro took the old man's advice and sliced off small portions which he swallowed, quite convinced that in doing so he had also swallowed a great many flies and he was quite certain that he could feel them flying around in his stomach. When he mentioned this to Scruffy, the old man just laughed and said that if he had had a dollar for every fly he had ever eaten he would have been a very rich man long ago.

It surprised Jethro just how quickly the temperature dropped once the sun had disappeared although he ought to have realized that it happened, having experienced similar but less severe drops in temperature as he and his family had crossed from the East, and they were soon forced to light a fire. Fortunately, there did not appear to be any shortage of dry sage and grass and a reasonable supply of more substantial wood, although Jethro could never make out where it had come from since the one thing which was very conspicuous by its absence, was a tree or even signs of trees having been there. Acting on Scruffy's advice, they lit the fire in the lee of a large rock, the idea being that the glow would be that much more difficult to see should anyone look out from the pass. In the light of the fire, Scruffy drew a rough map of Stillwater Pass and for the first time Jethro could see why it had acquired the name. If Scruffy's map was correct, there was a large lake near the top of the pass, a lake also known as Stillwater Lake. The trail apparently followed the eastern side of the lake since, according to Scruffy, the mountains came down almost sheer on the opposite side.

'Most likely place they is goin' to be is right here. . . .' Scruffy indicated the far end of the lake. 'There's a large, flat rock, almost an island, what juts out into the water which gives a good view of the whole lake. The water around the rock is pretty damned deep. I hear some say it's more'n five hundred feet deep just there. Don't know about that, maybe it is, maybe it ain't; all I know is it's too damned deep for the likes of me, I never did learn to swim. Can you swim, son?' Jethro nodded. 'Anyhow, even if you could swim across it's one hell of a climb. Only way across to the rock is a narrow neck of land about fifty yards long an' there ain't no cover. I even seen that under water once, but that was when we had one hell of a bad rainy season, which don't happen all that often. If they is on there they'd be almost impossible to get at.'

'Then what the hell are we doing this for?' grumbled Jethro. 'I only hope this isn't another wasted journey.' He gave a heavy sigh and shook his head. 'You just find them and I'll do the worrying about how to get at them. I can't decide on nothing until I know exactly where they are.'

Scruffy pointed at the map drawn in the dust again and added a few more lines and started to explain just how, in his opinion, they could reach the lake and rock without being seen, but most of what was being said seemed to become a distant drone as Jethro found himself nodding off. . . .

The night had been exceedingly cold and Jethro seemed to have spent most of it keeping the fire going. The horse and mule had positioned themselves as close to it as they could whilst Scruffy appeared to have slept right through and seemed surprised at Jethro's claim to have been awake most of the night.

'You want I should go over how we get up there again?' asked Scruffy. 'Seems to me you didn't take much notice last night.'

'I didn't,' admitted Jethro. 'I was too damned tired, I still am. No, you just lead the way and I'll follow.'

'It'll take maybe an hour to reach the mountains,' said Scruffy. 'It's all flat to there but after that it means a lot of climbin'.'

'It'll make a change from what we have been doing,' muttered Jethro. 'You just lead on, don't worry about what I can or can't do.' Before they left the pool they refilled the canteens and made sure that the animals had also had their fill.

For once Scruffy was correct in estimating how long it would take to reach the mountains – it was exactly one hour after leaving the pool. There was no gradual rise, the mountain suddenly rose almost sheer and to Jethro's inexperienced eye there did not appear to be any way upwards which their animals could negotiate. Scruffy, however, unerringly led the way through a series of fissures only wide enough for Jethro's horse and eventually the going became easier although it was very steep. Scruffy's mule appeared more at home in these surroundings than the horse.

It took the better part of an hour before the terrain began to level out as they made their way along a narrow track between two towering peaks and quite suddenly the lake came into view, perhaps some 400 feet below them. The large rock or island was clearly visible at the far end, although from that distance it was quite impossible to detect any signs of life on it. They eventually reached a point where the track twisted down towards the lake; but Scruffy indicated that it was now time to make a detour.

They left the main track, taking what appeared to be nothing more than a faint animal track off to the right and started to climb upwards again, although they did not climb very high before reaching what appeared to be a natural ring of rock a few hundred feet below the mountain peaks which seemed to stretch all around what appeared to be a large, deep hole. Jethro had heard of volcano craters and wondered if this was one, but when he questioned Scruffy on the matter the old man did not even seem to know what a volcano was.

Apart from two areas of loose scree, their progress was unhindered and about an hour after leaving the main track they were high above the large rock and studying it intently. Eventually their studying paid off as Scruffy nudged his companion and pointed downwards.

'There they is!' he whispered, as if afraid that the sound of his voice would reach those below, even though they were at least 500 feet above them and almost half a mile away. Jethro strained his eyes and finally located the men. He grunted with a certain amount of satisfaction, relieved that the long trip and hard work had apparently been worth the effort.

'It looks like them,' he agreed. 'There's three of them and they seem to have made a proper camp as if they intend to be there some time. All I have to do now is get down there and surprise them.'

'The best thing you can do is come at them from the other side,' said Scruffy. 'If they is expectin' us at all they'll be expectin' us along the trail from the other end of the lake.'

'And they'll be expecting horses,' nodded Jethro. 'I say we leave the horse and the mule up here and go in on foot.' He took his rifle from the saddle holster, checked that both it and his handgun were loaded and took a box of ammunition from his saddle-bag. 'What about you,' he asked Scruffy, 'are you joining the party?'

'I wouldn't miss it for anythin' in the world,' laughed Scruffy. 'Follow me, I know the best way down.'

Although steep, the descent was not too difficult and about half an hour later they were at the lakeside with the rock about 300 yards away. There was plenty of cover in the form of stunted trees and thick brush, the only difficult part being a stretch of about fifty yards leading up to the narrow strip of land stretching out to the rock. It was here that they saw the three men sitting on some rocks apparently looking down the trail. Jethro studied the area for some time and eventually decided that it would be quite impossible to approach even from their direction without being seen. He even thought about using his rifle there and then, but realized that he might succeed in shooting only one of them and even then without any guarantee of accuracy.

'The one place they certainly won't be expecting anyone to come from would be the rock itself,' he said to Scruffy.

'And the only way you can do that is by swimmin' across to it,' said Scruffy. 'You can count me out on that; like I said, I can't swim.'

'Well, unless they move there isn't any other way,'

said Jethro. 'Anyhow, it might be good idea if you stayed here to create a diversion if necessary.'

'Suits me,' agreed Scruffy. 'I already had me my bath for this year.' Jethro resisted the temptation to make the observation that it had probably been well in excess of a year since Scruffy's body had had any water anywhere near it, judging by the smell emitted by the old man.

Leaving Scruffy where he was, Jethro made his way back to the lake where he stood behind a rock and studied the distance between him and his objective which at that point was about 150 yards. Suddenly the distance appeared rather daunting and although Jethro could swim, he had never attempted anything of that distance before. There was also the problem of keeping both his rifle and handgun out of the water and relatively dry. Another problem became very evident when he tested the water.

He shuddered slightly as he dipped in his arm and discovered it to be freezing cold and he began to have very serious doubts about the feasibility of his plan. He also felt the injuries to his shoulder and arm and wondered if he would have the strength to both swim and support his guns. The possibility of an assault from the narrow strip joining the rock to the land now seemed rather more attractive, but after giving it some further thought he realized that such an approach would be doomed to failure and since he had come this far and expended so much effort, he was not inclined to chance failure in any form. Eventually, he decided to get closer to the rock and swim. Keeping a wary eye on the three men now with their backs towards him, he moved closer until the distance across to the rock was only about sixty yards, removed his shirt and wrapped his guns in it and slowly waded into the lake, gasping for breath as the cold water hit his body. . . .

NINE

The water was very soon up to Jethro's neck and for
a few moments he could not move, the extreme cold-
ness of the water making it very difficult to breathe.
As his body slowly became acclimatized to the
temperature, he very nearly abandoned the idea, but
a quick glance in the direction of the three men, still
with their backs towards him, hardened his resolve.
Thoughts of vengeance very quickly blotted out any
feeling of cold or discomfort and he struck out
towards the rock, trying to keep his guns, wrapped in
his shirt, clear of the water. However, try as he might,
the shirt quickly became soaked, but he persevered
even though the weight of the guns seemed to
increase with each stroke.

Under normal circumstances, a swim of about
sixty yards would have presented no problems, but
the cold, the awkwardness of the guns and the need
for extreme quiet turned that short distance into
something of a marathon. More than once he
stopped swimming and held his breath as one of the
men turned round and appeared to be looking
straight at him, but he obviously had not been seen

as they would turn their attention back to the others.

How long the swim took, Jethro really had no idea except that it seemed to last far longer than he would have expected. Eventually, however, he felt his feet touch bottom as he neared the rock and was grateful to be able to transfer his weight and energy to his legs even though they were numb with cold. He did not leave the water straight away, preferring to make his way further round the rock until he was quite certain that he was out of sight of the three men. He could now see that it was in fact a series of rocks and not a single rock as Scruffy had indicated.

Eventually he slowly waded to the base of the rocks and into a small recess which seemed to offer the best way up, although nowhere was that easy. Although not particularly high, the rock face was sheer and seemed to offer few foot or hand-holds. This particular recess at least seemed to have the advantage of there being a small ledge about a foot above the water. After quietly placing his guns on the ledge, he managed to haul himself out of the water and the first thing he did was check the mechanisms of his weapons. He breathed a sigh of relief when everything appeared to be in order.

Since time appeared to be on his side, Jethro did not attempt to climb up the remaining fifteen feet or so straight away, opting instead to rub vigorously at his cold, aching limbs in an effort to restore some circulation into them. This process took longer than he had anticipated – perhaps fifteen minutes – during which time his clothes dried out to a certain extent. He replaced his shirt and stood up to survey the rock behind him, noting with dismay that it appeared to be perfectly smooth and did not offer much chance of an easy climb. However, he noted that the recess in which he now was, narrowed into what appeared to be a round chimney shape which, apart from the first few feet, could be climbed by placing his back against one wall and bracing his feet against the other. Access to the point where this was possible was not so easy.

There was just one fairly deep-looking crack in the rock into which his hands would have slipped quite easily, but this was about two feet out of his reach. He thought about jumping up to it but knew that one slip would have sent him crashing into the water and, apart from being heard, could well have caused him severe injury on any one of the many jagged rocks just below the surface of the water. His eye caught sight of a fairly large rock on the edge of the ledge and he attempted to move it so that he could stand on it and thus reach the crack, but from where he was, it proved impossible to move, although it was plainly loose.

After studying the situation for a few minutes, he decided that the only way he was going to move the rock was to once again stand in the water from where he could get a better grip to lever it along the ledge. Placing his precious weapons carefully out of the line of movement, he gingerly lowered himself into the water and, although still icy cold, he thought that it did not seem quite as cold as before.

Even from his position in the water, the rock proved very difficult to move. After struggling with it for about five minutes, he peered between a crack and saw that a small sliver of rock seemed to be blocking movement. He always carried a knife, but even the blade of it, although touching the sliver, could not dislodge it. He looked about for something else and saw a small branch floating in the water about three or four yards out. There seemed to be no alternative to swimming the few yards. This time the iciness of the water really did hit him once again.

With his prize in hand, Jethro gasped for breath as he once again set to dislodging the offending sliver of rock and for a moment it seemed that he had succeeded, but at the vital moment the thin branch snapped. Once again he inserted the shortened branch, at first dislodging the previously broken piece and then managing to get it round the top of the sliver. To his great relief the piece of rock slid to one side making it possible to insert the blade of his knife and slowly pull it clear.

Once again he pushed and lifted at the rock and this time it moved, although it proved a lot heavier than he had anticipated. Eventually he was able to manoeuvre it into the position he wanted and once again clambered on to the ledge, picked up his guns, placing the pistol in its holster and jamming the rifle through his belt. By standing on the rock, the crack above was now just within reach.

The cold seemed to have taken its toll on his strength; normally he would have had no difficulty in hauling himself the two or three feet to the point where he could brace his back against the rock, but it took three attempts before he breathlessly forced his numbed body into position, where he stayed for a few minutes to recover. Eventually he began the slow process of ascending the chimney.

The top of the chimney was reached some ten minutes later and he spent another ten minutes lying flat, recovering his strength, checking his guns yet again and listening. The one thing that Scruffy had not been able to tell him was just where on the rock the men were likely to have made their camp and, after recovering his strength and composure, he began to look about. The snort of a horse made him peer over what seemed to be the highest part of the rock where he saw a makeshift camp and three horses. Plainly if the horses were there there must have been a fairly easy way round. However, there was no sign of the men and he had to assume that they were still sitting on the narrow spit of land joining the rock to the shore. He slowly made his way across the rock, which proved a lot bigger than he had expected, taking care not to make even the slightest noise, although once or twice he froze and waited expectantly as his feet did slip. Eventually he was overlooking the narrow strip of land between the rock and the shore and the sight which greeted him was entirely unexpected. . . .

'Dinner!' declared Ernie Johnson, pointing across the strip of land. The object of his attention was a small deer which had ventured down to the lake for a drink, apparently unaware of the three men.

Ernie grabbed his rifle and, closely followed by Humpback Chisholm, attempted to get closer to the animal, but it sensed their presence and before either of them could take aim, it bounded away towards some thick bushes. Suddenly it stopped, flicked its tail and jerked its head and then bounded off in the opposite direction.

'Somethin' spooked it,' said Humpback. 'As far as

I know there ain't no mountain lions up here an' that's about the only thing as'd spook a deer in these parts.'

'Exceptin' maybe a human bein',' grunted Ernie. 'You ever had the feelin' you was bein' watched? I had me this feelin' for a long time now, but I just put it down to imagination, now I ain't so sure.'

'Sure, I know what you mean,' nodded Humpback. 'Can't say as I felt it this time, but I have in the past. That could explain me hearin' what I thought was a horse snortin' somewhere up the hill some time ago, but I put that down to an echo from our horses.'

'There's one way to find out,' whispered Ernie. 'You go along the edge of the water as far as that big tree an' I'll head up towards that pointed rock. . . .' He indicated a needle-shaped rock on the edge of the bushes. 'Give me a couple of minutes an' then close in. I'd say whoever it is is over by that old thorn tree.'

The pair split up and less than two minutes later, Humpback Chisholm triumphantly emerged from the bushes pushing a dirty, twisted figure in front of him. About two minutes later he was joined by Ernie Price.

'There don't seem to be nobody else,' said Ernie, 'but I don't see Sam bein' on his own, he wouldn't have the guts to come after us alone.'

'Then that bastard Jethro Smith must be around somewhere,' hissed Humpback, gripping his rifle and looking about. 'OK, Sam, where the hell is he?'

'How the hell should I know,' growled Scruffy. 'A man's allowed to come up here if'n he wants to, ain't he? I been up here lots of times, probably more'n you. I didn't know you was here.'

'Liar!' snarled his brother. 'I knows when you is lyin', Sam, don't forget that. You got some explainin' to do; Pete'll be pleased to see you, that bastard Smith put a bullet through his neck.' Angrily he pushed Scruffy along towards the strip joining the shore and the rock, where Pete Watson was already walking towards them.

'I thought there was a funny stink around,' sneered Pete Watson. 'Is he alone?'

'We ain't found nobody else,' admitted Ernie, 'but I have me this feelin' that his new buddy, Jethro Smith, ain't too far away.'

'More'n like,' grunted Pete. 'OK, Sam, so how did you get this side of us without bein' seen? You sure didn't come along the trail, that's for sure.'

'There's ways,' rasped Scruffy.

'An' there's ways of makin' you talk!' threatened Ernie. 'It'll give me great pleasure in makin' you scream for mercy.'

'Where's Smith?' demanded Pete Watson, thrusting his face close to Scruffy's but quickly drawing back in disgust. 'You stink!' he hissed. 'Where is he, or do I have to let Ernie loose on you? You know just how mean Ernie can be, you wouldn't want him to hurt you, would you?'

'You can all go shit!' grated Scruffy, defiantly.

'It'll be the shit that'll be runnin' out of you before I'm finished with you,' rasped Ernie. 'Now, answer the question. Where is Smith?'

'Don't know,' hissed Scruffy, with a certain amount of truth.

'But he is, or was, with you?' prompted Humpback.

Scruffy faltered slightly which was as good as admitting that he was. 'I ain't seen him,' he insisted defiantly, desperately hoping that Jethro was at that moment taking aim.

'OK,' grinned Pete, 'If you want it the hard way, then the hard way you get it.' He nodded to Ernie who grinned evilly, placed his hands together and cracked his finger joints. Suddenly he lashed out, his fist sinking into Scruffy's thin stomach, making him double up in agony and, as he did so, his knee came up and smashed into his face.

'That's just a taster,' Ernie laughed. Scruffy was dragged from the ground by his brother and Ernie prepared to hit him once again. . . .

The shot echoed around the rocks and Ernie Price fell to the ground clutching at his upper chest. Scruffy was allowed to fall as Humpback and Pete Watson also crashed to the ground desperately looking for cover. There were two more shots, both of which ricocheted off rocks close to Humpback's head.

'Now we know just where he is!' panted Pete Watson, rubbing the side of his neck and wincing slightly. 'This time he really is mine.'

'Not if I see him first,' said Humpback.

'What I want to know is just how the hell did he get there?' rasped Ernie, drawing his hand across the top of his chest and looking ruefully at the blood which covered it.

'Just how don't matter none,' said Pete. 'The point is he is an' as it's turned out it's probably just about sealed his fate. We've got him trapped; there ain't nowhere else for him to go.'

Humpback kicked out at his brother who was now lying, apparently unconscious, close by. 'You did a good job on him,' he whispered to Ernie, 'he's out cold.'

'How bad is it?' Pete asked Ernie.

'Bad enough but it didn't do any serious damage,' replied Ernie.

Jethro's grip on his rifle tightened when he saw the unmistakable figure of Scruffy Chisholm being pushed along the spit of land towards the other unmistakable figure of Pete Watson. His immediate reaction was to raise the rifle and shoot Pete Watson, but even though the feeling of revenge was very deep rooted and it was his ultimate intention to kill all three men, he could not stop his mind and conscience revolting at the thought of shooting someone in the back and in cold blood.

'Naw!' he said to himself. 'Killing him like that would make you no better than they are, even if nobody else knew, you would and that's all that matters.' He lowered the gun and waited.

He did not have long to wait as Scruffy was pushed in front of Pete Watson and words were plainly exchanged. Suddenly Ernie Price straightened himself and his fist slammed into Scruffy's stomach. Jethro did not actually see Ernie's knee smash into Scruffy's face, but he knew what had happened. When Humpback Chisholm bent down and dragged his brother off the ground and once again Ernie Price prepared to swing his fist, all thoughts of shooting an unarmed and defenceless man had disappeared from his mind as he quickly brought the rifle to his shoulder. . . .

*

'We know just where you are, Smith!' called Pete
Watson. 'There ain't no way off that rock unless you
want a cold swim.'

'How do you think I got here?' responded Jethro.
'I haven't learnt how to fly yet, but I'm working on it.'

'That figures,' called Pete Watson again. 'You sure
didn't cross on foot. The thing is, Mr Clever Sod,
you've just swum yourself into a perfect trap. We
know you're there now an' we've got all the time in
the world, which is more'n you have. We can sit here
for a month if we have to, how long can you last out?'

'I've got plenty of horse meat,' laughed Jethro,
more out of a sense of bravado than actual intent.

'OK,' conceded Watson. 'The thing is you have to
sleep sometime. There's three of us remember; you
hit Ernie all right, but nothin' too serious. We can
take it in turns to sleep an' don't think you can fool
us again by swimmin' back. We know your horse must
be up the hillside somewheres, Humpy is goin' up
there to find it.'

For the first time Jethro realized that in trying to
protect Scruffy, he had put himself into a very difficult position, although he refused to admit defeat.

There followed a long period of silence as Jethro
weighed up his position and he suddenly decided to
take the risk of slipping back to where the men had
left their horses, reasonably certain that none of
them would attempt anything since they did not
know just where he was.

A quick examination of their equipment showed
that one of them did not have a rifle, that still being
in a saddle holster and he had to assume that it

belonged to Pete Watson. A search of their saddle-bags also produced several boxes of ammunition so he was reasonably certain that what they had with them was all they had access to. He quickly returned to his spot overlooking the three and, as expected, it appeared that they had not moved. He had been away for less than five minutes.

'You haven't got that much ammunition,' Jethro called out. 'I reckon I can last out longer than you.'

'We'll see!' called Pete Watson.

'He's gone very quiet,' whispered Humpback. 'I reckon he's moved. I'm goin' to take a look.'

'It's your funeral,' hissed Ernie Price. 'I'm for stayin' right here until sundown, then we can move.'

Humpback looked a little scornfully at his companions and stood up very slowly and even he had to express some surprise when there was no shot. He moved surprisingly quickly behind a large rock partly in the water and waited. A short time later Jethro's voice boomed out from somewhere very close by.

'It appears to me that we have something of a stale-mate,' called Jethro.

'*You* have a stalemate,' laughed Watson. 'Come nightfall we can just walk out of here or we can come across there. The thing is, if we do walk out of here, you won't know where we are. You won't be able to walk past a rock or a tree without wonderin' if one of us is behind it. It could be you'll feel a bullet almost as soon as you leave or it could be a couple of days, it all depends on how we feel.'

Jethro realized that Pete Watson was correct; he had, by his hasty actions, placed himself in a very awkward situation, but in some ways he did not regret what had happened, he could not have stood by and watched while they beat Scruffy Chisholm to a pulp or even killed him.

There was a slight noise somewhere behind Jethro which he put down to coming from one of the three horses, but suddenly he was very aware that it was something more than that and he twisted round, Colt in hand, just as a shot thudded into the ground where his head had been a second earlier. Acting by pure reaction and an instinct for self-preservation, he squeezed the trigger and saw the distorted figure of Humpback Chisholm drop his rifle as he fell. There followed a splash as the body hit the water.

'One less!' called Jethro. 'That leaves just the two of you.'

'I told him he was mad!' came the voice of Ernie Price. 'That still don't get you off there, Smith.'

Jethro was actually rather pleased with the way he had reacted and the apparent accuracy of his shooting and could not resist the temptation to go over to the point where Humpback Chisholm had fallen into the water, but rather to his disappointment, there was nothing to be seen, no body floating on the water and certainly no sign of an injured man on the rocks. He thought that he could just make out something floating below the surface and convinced himself that it was Chisholm's body. He quickly returned to his position overlooking the remaining men and, after double checking, was certain that both were still there. The body of Scruffy Chisholm still lay where it had fallen and Jethro wondered if the old man had died.

The standoff continued until just before sunset,

during which time Jethro adopted the ploy of remaining competely silent, refusing to answer or react to the frequent questions and taunts which were hurled his way. His reasoning was quite simple: by remaining silent he hoped to unnerve the two remaining men and as the hours wore on it was quite obvious that this strategy was having some effect if the tone of their questioning and taunts was anything to go by.

During all that time there had been no movement from Scruffy Chisholm and the feeling that the old man had died grew into certainty but, about half an hour before sunset, the old man's legs moved and Jethro heard a groan. He was pleased that Scruffy was still alive, but it did appear that he must have been badly injured by the blow to the stomach. Pete Watson called out to tell Jethro that the old man was still alive, but Jethro still maintained his silence.

Darkness came quite suddenly; one minute the sun could be seen just above the mountain tops and the next it had disappeared and the whole area plunged into almost total blackness, almost but not quite, Jethro could still make out where the men were. It was a further fifteen minutes before the light had disappeared completely.

Jethro realized that he could not simply sit and wait all night; that would place him in the same position he had been most of that day and he thought it most unlikely that either of the men would make a move in his direction. After listening intently for a few minutes and detecting nothing, cautiously and very slowly he raised himself and, taking care to feel his way and to make as little sound as possible, he inched his way down the rocks to where he knew the men to be.

Twenty minutes later he found the body of Scruffy Chisholm but no sign of the other two. He was not surprised; on the way down he had convinced himself that they would make use of the cover of darkness to make good their escape and head for somewhere where they had better control of the situation.

Scruffy was still alive, although he was certainly in no condition to communicate and Jethro moved him to the lee of a rock and, remembering that there were at least three blankets where the men had made camp, made his way back and eventually returned and covered Scruffy with two of them. The third he used himself, settling down for the night on the basis that it was too dark for either himself or Watson and Price to attempt anything. He even considered lighting a fire, but very quickly discarded the idea, although as that night wore on he reconsidered this more than once.

It appeared that Watson and Price had other ideas about sleeping. Just as Jethro had settled down he was subjected to a barrage of taunts and abuse from somewhere apparently not too far away, although he continued his policy of maintaining complete silence. After about an hour this seemed to pay off and they lapsed into silence. For the remainder of the night all he had to contend with was the cold and frequent checks on Scruffy's state of health.

TEN

Jethro was up before dawn, simply guessing at what time it was. His first action was to check on the condition of Scruffy, whom he found to be still alive, although his breathing was becoming more and more laboured. It was obvious even to his untrained eye that Scruffy urgently needed the services of a doctor. For a few moments he looked into the blackness in the direction he assumed Watson and Price to be and then once again felt Scruffy's chest. His mind was made up, the most important thing at that moment was to get the old man back to Henderson and Doc Galloway.

However, he was quite certain that Watson and Price would do their best to ensure that he never achieved that objective but he also felt that he had to make some sort of move in order to force the two men to do something. He would have to take the chance on what that something might be. He would have liked very much to have found his own horse, Albert, but knew that he had no choice but to use the animals left by Watson and Price. If he came through successfully or there was somehow some time later on, he would return to find Albert, in the meantime he knew that the animal was in no immediate danger.

Fumbling his way in the darkness to where the three horses were was not too difficult and he managed to saddle two of them, deciding that he would leave the third horse to fend for itself, having made sure that it was free so to do. Leading the two animals back proved a little more difficult as they continually shied and pulled as they picked their way between rocks. Eventually, however, Jethro had them on the spit of land where, although it was still dark, he somehow managed to haul Scruffy into the saddle of one of them. He was quite certain that he had aggravated the old man's injury even more, but at that moment there was nothing he could do about it, there was no other way for him to travel. He managed to strap Scruffy into the saddle and used the three rolled-up blankets to prop his front. He just had to hope that this crude arrangement served its purpose. He then mounted the other horse and checked that both his guns were loaded and still in working order before gently urging his horse forward whilst leading the other. It was still completely dark and he began to have doubts as to just how close to dawn it really was especially as it was so cold, although he was reasonably certain that it was not too far away.

Once across the spit of land he headed out along where he had seen the trail, although his sense of direction was mainly by pure instinct and allowing the horse to make its own way naturally. He was more than surprised when, after a few minutes, he had not been shot at although it was still very dark and knew that he would not have attempted anything, but he was still surprised.

Just like the sunset the previous evening, sunrise came very suddenly; he had been able to make out some shapes for a few minutes when the sun broke over the mountains and everything became perfectly clear apart from a few long shadows. Instinctively he loosened the gun in his gunbelt and drew the rifle out of the saddle holster and then watched, listened and waited. . . .

He had no more than five minutes to wait before a shot suddenly echoed around and he sensed a bullet pass close to his head, although he was quite certain that it had missed him since he felt no pain and a quick check revealed no blood, but he had heard of cases where someone had been hit and not known it. Throwing himself from his horse in a deliberate attempt to make it look as though he had been hit, Jethro landed on the ground, allowing his rifle to drop to one side to make his fall look more realistic at the same time making sure that his Colt was in his hand. The horses shied and moved on a short distance and Jethro held his breath hoping that he had done the right thing.

There was a brief pause before he sensed rather than saw Watson and Price emerge from some bushes and for a few anxious moments he braced himself against the half-expected bullet fired to make certain that he was dead. Fortunately, that bullet never arrived and he heard the crunch of leather on the sand and stones as the men approached. His grip tightened on the gun in his hand but he did not move.

'Is he dead?' Jethro heard Pete Watson ask. 'Pity if he is, I'd've liked to have made him die real slow to make him pay for all the trouble he's caused. A quick death is too good for him.'

'Don't see no blood,' grunted Ernie Price, as he crouched beside Jethro.

'That's because you missed!' snarled Jethro, twisting slightly and ramming his Colt into Ernie's chest at the same time squeezing the trigger. There was a muffled explosion and, in the same instant, he pulled Ernie on top of him to give himself protection. The breath rattled noisily in Ernie's throat and chest for a few seconds but it appeared that Jethro's bullet had hit Ernie's heart as the body went limp. In what was nothing more than pure instinct, Jethro pushed his hand and gun around the body and moved his head just in time to see Pete Watson taking careful aim. There was only one shot and Pete Watson crumpled slowly to the ground. Jethro remained under the weight of Ernie Price until he was quite certain that Pete Watson was not going to move again before pushing the body to one side and struggling to his feet, his gun ready for use just in case Watson was still alive. He checked on the condition of both men and was finally quite certain that both were dead. For the first time Jethro allowed himself the luxury of a very satisfied grin. At last his parents and sister had been avenged.

There was no thought about taking the bodies back to Henderson and he was quite certain that Sheriff Wally Hutchinson would not really have appreciated it had he done so. He had learned that Wally was much happier if he simply did not know about certain things. Nor was there any thought about burying the bodies; as far as he was concerned they could suffer the same fate as they had dispensed to his family, to rot in the heat of the sun. A groan from Scruffy made him remember what was now the most important thing, although he doubted if anyone in Henderson would have been too bothered if Scruffy Chisholm also simply disappeared.

However, now that it was light, he thought that he was very close to where they had left Albert and Scruffy's mule and decided that a few minutes was not going to make much difference to Scruffy's condition. He left Scruffy still in the saddle but under the shade of a tree and turned up the hill in search of his horse and the mule. Twenty minutes later he returned leading both animals, tied them, along with the horse Scruffy was on, to his saddle and made his way back in the direction of Henderson, hoping that he could find his way. One thing of which he was quite certain was that should Scruffy die on the journey, he would not even bother to go back to Henderson even though his wagon and all his worldly goods were still there. Even the thought of the land certificate no longer seemed important; he was not at all sure that he now wanted to take up life as a farmer, although farming was all he knew.

By travelling non-stop apart from a brief few minutes mainly for the benefit of the animals at muddy water-hole, Jethro reached Henderson in the early hours of the morning; three o'clock in the morning, according to a very disgruntled Doc Galloway when he answered the persistent hammering on his door. Scruffy Chisholm was taken inside and examined and the doc pronounced that one of the old man's

ribs had punctured his lungs and that it was touch
and go as to whether or not he would survive. In any
event, an operation would have to be performed to
straighten out the rib and to repair the damage to
the lung. Jethro left Scruffy in what he considered
very capable hands, despite the warning that the old
man could just as easily die during the operation. He
then went along to his own wagon and went to bed,
deciding that what he had to say to Wally Hutchinson
could remain unsaid until a more civilized hour.

'Doc Galloway called me,' grumbled Wally. 'It looks
like you got Sam Chisholm back just in time, the doc
reckons he's goin' to be all right.'

'You don't sound too pleased,' remarked Jethro.

'Don't matter none to me one way or the other,'
shrugged the sheriff. 'The doc also reckons his ribs
were broken by someone hittin' him. Now I can't see
you doin' a thing like that so I have to assume that
you must've met up with Pete Watson. . . .' Jethro
nodded. 'That bein' the case,' continued Wally, 'I'm
surprised you're still alive. That also bein' the case,
unless you're a ghost, which I don't believe you are,
I'd say that Pete Watson, Ernie Price an' Humpback
Chisholm are now buzzard meat. . . .' Once again
Jethro nodded. 'Don't tell me no more, son,' said
Wally, almost pleading with Jethro. 'I might not like
what I hear. Now, since there ain't nothin' to keep
you here no more, when are you leavin'?'

'You make that sound more like an order than a
question,' smiled Jethro. 'OK, I can take a hint as
well as the next man. I'll be on my way first thing
tomorrow.'

'That long,' muttered Wally, as if he were complaining. 'OK, son, I ain't forcin' you out of town, you understand,' he said almost apologetically, 'but I'll be mighty glad to get Henderson back to somethin' like normality. That's somethin' that's been sadly lackin' ever since you rode in.'

'Things haven't been exactly what I would call normal as far as I'm concerned either,' replied Jethro. 'I had me a family until I got here.'

'Yeh,' muttered Wally self-consciously. 'Sorry about that, I wasn't thinkin'.'

'That's OK,' said Jethro. 'Anyhow, I'll be glad to be on my way, I have some land to claim.'

'Take my advice, son,' grinned Wally. 'As soon as you've staked your claim, you take time out to find yourself a good woman. Any amount of land ain't no use unless there's a good woman somewhere.'

'I hear what you say,' grinned Jethro, 'but I am only nineteen; there's plenty of time for things like that.'

'Get the best while you're young enough,' grinned Wally.

'I'll try to remember that,' smiled Jethro. 'It sounds to me like you might have a few ladies in mind.'

'There's a couple,' nodded Wally.

'Maybe there are,' said Jethro, 'but if you don't mind that is one thing I'd like to make my own decision about and it certainly won't be for some time yet.'

'Just tryin' to be helpful,' smiled Wally.

Jethro left the sheriff and went to see the Reverend and Mrs Gough, who seemed genuinely relieved that he had returned safely. He explained what had happened and, although obviously saddened, the reverend did not condemn him. Mrs Gough insisted that he had a good breakfast, maintaining that the food at Grace Stallard's was unfit for human consumption and Jethro was heartily in agreement with her on that. He offered to give Albert and the saddle back to them but this was very firmly rejected and he did not argue too much.

The remainder of the morning was spent in cleaning out the wagon, buying stores and equipment and refilling the two water butts strapped to the side of the wagon. His mules appeared to be in good condition even though they had been left to their own devices almost the whole of the time he had been in Henderson. Eventually, well supplied and satisfied that everything was in order and since he felt that it was too late to think about leaving that day, he wandered along to check on the condition of Scruffy Chisholm.

'He certainly smells better,' said Mrs Galloway, as she showed Jethro into the small bedroom. 'I took the opportunity to give him a good cleaning all over. I honestly don't think that body of his has seen soap and water for a good many years. There's some stains no amount of scrubbing will remove.'

'He should be all right,' said Doc Galloway. 'The damage to his lung was not as bad as I thought it would be, but even so you got him back just in time. I don't think he would've lasted more than another day at the most.'

Scruffy himself appeared completely unaware of his visitor and Jethro made no attempt to wake him, saying that he would call in again later.

During the morning, Jethro had been amazed at

just how quickly stories about him and the Watson gang had spread. Most of them were wildly off the mark, ranging from a shoot out at the caves on Payute Flats to Jethro murdering them in cold blood, although one particular story was so near what actually happened that he wondered if someone had been witness to the incident. He was never able to discover just who it was started that story. Nevertheless, it was generally accepted that Pete Watson and his gang were now dead and most people now treated Jethro with a great deal of respect in spite of his young age and even though he was not wearing his gun around the town. He even overheard one or two mothers threatening their children with letting him deal with the errant offspring, a threat which seemed to have some effect.

The heat of the afternoon was avoided by spending most of it asleep in his wagon despite the continual buzz of timber being sawn in the nearby sawmill and a very persistent group of children congregating nearby taunting him, challenging him to come out and shoot them. There were a few moments when he very nearly accepted their challenge.

When he returned to see Scruffy, still at Doc Galloway's despite Mrs Galloway's assertion that he would have to be moved back to his own shack, the old man was awake and smiled broadly as Jethro entered the room.

'We made it!' he croaked. 'Unless I'm in Heaven, we must've made it.'

'I would say that Heaven is one place you will never see,' laughed Jethro. 'Sure, we made it, they're all dead.'

'Last thing I remember is Ernie Price hittin' me,'

said Scruffy. 'I thought then my end had come an' I didn't give much for your chances either.'

'Frankly, neither did I,' admitted Jethro. 'Anyway, from now on you won't have that brother of yours to bother you.'

'Yeh,' sighed Scruffy. 'I've been thinkin' about that, maybe I shouldn't've hated him the way I did, after all, we was twins. I even feel like I've lost part of myself. Anyhow, I can't thank you enough for gettin' me back here an' savin' my life, the doc tells me it was touch an' go. I reckon Hal Morgan, the veterinarian would've made a better job of stitchin' me up though.'

'You were not in any condition to say who stitched you up,' reminded Jethro. 'The doc tells me the bill is twenty dollars so far. I reckon that's one bill you can pay yourself, I think I've paid more than enough one way or another. In fact I think you should be paying me for what I have done so far.'

Scruffy smiled and nodded. 'If it's money you want, son,' he said, 'I've got me a bit put by, you're welcome to some of it. Old Sam Chisholm ain't as badly off as most folk think, I made sure of that.'

'By scrounging off others!' laughed Jethro.

'That was expected,' grinned Scruffy. 'It kind of grew into a habit. but it did save me a few dollars.'

'And I don't think you'll change much,' said Jethro. 'Anyhow, I thought I'd better tell you that I'm leaving in the morning. I can't say that it's been a pleasure knowing you, but it has certainly been an experience. I don't expect we will ever meet again and I can't say that I particularly want to either.'

'I guess that goes for me too, son,' smiled Scruffy.

'Anyhow, thanks for what you did an' I'm only sorry that it took the murder of your folks to get you involved.'

'Me too!' said Jethro, solemnly.

His next call was to the cemetery where he stood at the foot of the three graves for some considerable time, some of it in silent prayer and the remainder of the time in talking in a low voice to the three people buried there, explaining everything that had happened and why, as if seeking their approval or even forgiveness.

'This is the last time I shall be able to come and see you,' he said, almost apologetically. 'I found that land certificate, Pa, I guess it's up to me to claim it now. I'm not too sure that farming is what I really want to do now though, I'll have to think about it. Still, I guess owning a piece of land is almost as good as money in the bank, so I reckon I will claim it and then think about it. You won't be neglected though, the Reverend and Mrs Gough have promised to look after you. They're good folk, he was a sheriff once, but then I guess you know all that now. In fact, I guess you know everything that has happened, so I guess I was wasting my time telling you.' He looked at his sister's grave and nodded. 'You make sure you look after Ma and Pa in their old age, assuming there is such a thing as old age where you are. Anyhow, you just look after them.'

He wiped a tear from his eye and turned away, sad that it would be the last time he would see the graves. He paused by the gate, looked briefly back, straightened his shoulders and walked proudly up the street, determined that he would never do anything of which his parents or his sister would disapprove.

*

It had been his intention to turn in early that evening, but it seemed hotter than usual and after a fruitless hour trying to sleep, he finally got up and decided that perhaps a couple of whiskies might help induce that elusive state.

The saloon was as busy as it usually was, although when he entered a sudden silence fell on the room and its occupants and everyone stared at him for some time as if expecting him to do something. When it became apparent that he had come in only for a drink, everyone gradually turned their attention back to what they had been doing.

'You've earned yourself quite a reputation,' smiled Jimmy, the bartender. 'I know there's one or two of the younger ones who've been weighin' up their chances of takin' you on.'

'What the hell for?' sighed Jethro. 'That kind of thing doesn't prove anything and could mean you end up dead.'

'You know how kids are,' shrugged Jimmy. 'They want to prove that they're better'n anyone else.'

'And I've proved it?' asked Jethro. 'I'm not much more than a kid myself.'

'Guess not,' admitted Jimmy. 'The thing is you have proved it and they haven't and nor are they likely to in Henderson. Maybe it's good thing you're leavin' town; I reckon you might've proved irresistible to one or two an' that would've been a pity since I'm pretty sure who would've won after seein' you perform against Watson an' Higgins.'

'Then I agree, it is as well I am leaving.'

'The thing is,' continued Jimmy, 'out here a man

who is good with his gun can either be somethin' of a god or the target for every tearaway; mostly he's the target for tearaways. Once you've earned a reputation it seems to follow you around an' other would-be gunfighters seem to sense it just like a fly senses a pile of shit an' they all come out of the wood-work. Take my advice, keep it as quiet as possible.'

'I will,' said Jethro, actually feeling quite proud that he had built up a reputation, especially in such a short time, but he also accepted what Jimmy was trying to tell him. He had no first-hand experience but he had heard stories.

Quite suddenly, an elderly man burst into the room, looking wildly about and, seeing Jethro, shouted to him.

'I thought you said you'd killed 'em all!' he shouted. 'Well, unless I just seen a ghost, which I don't think I have, then you ain't.'

'I don't remember telling anyone else but the sheriff what happened,' said Jethro. 'What are you talking about?'

'Humpback Chisholm is what I'm talkin' about,' barked the man, flinging his arms wildly in the direc-tion of the door. 'I just seen him ride over the bridge.'

'Where is he now?' demanded Jimmy.

'Don't know,' hissed the man. 'I didn't hang about long enough to find out. Anyhow, I've told you an' right now I'm gettin' the hell out of here.'

Most of the other customers of the saloon also decided that they had had enough drink for one night and hastily gathered their belongings and disappeared, some through the front door but most by the back in the direction of the privy. A few others licked their lips a little apprehensively and doggedly stayed where they were, anxious not to miss anything. It was noticeable that all the young men Jimmy had been talking about had also disappeared with the others.

'Have you got your gun?' Jimmy asked, peering over the counter and, on seeing that Jethro was unarmed, he bent under the counter and produced a rather worn gunbelt and a battered-looking Adams pistol. 'Better put this on,' he urged. 'It ain't what you're used to, but it's better'n nothin'. Just remember it's only a five shot and don't pack the punch of a Colt.'

'And you think I'll need it?' asked Jethro.

'The choice is yours,' grunted Jimmy. 'If Humpback is in town it's a certain fact just who he'll be after and remember that he knows how to handle a gun as well.'

'OK!' sighed Jethro. 'But I think he must've been seeing things; I saw Humpback Chisholm drown. I shot him myself, so it can't be him.'

'I hope you're right,' said Jimmy. 'Now, put it on before whoever it is comes in here, he sure won't wait for you if you don't.'

That, at least, was logical; whoever it was, if they were intent on killing him, certainly would not wait while he donned his gunbelt. Jethro fastened the belt and then tested the Adams for weight, pulled a face and then checked on the chambers. Finding the gun loaded, he slipped it into the holster and then attempted a quick draw which to his mind was not fast enough but to the onlookers appeared very fast. Two more decided that they would be better off out of the room.

'Where's Wally Hutchinson?' Jethro asked. 'He ought to be here doing something.'

'Tonight is the night Wally goes along to the Fletcher place along with one or two others,' explained Jimmy. 'They say they go to make music, you know, a band. Wally plays the fiddle, pretty damned good at it too an' the others play things like banjo, accordion an' flute. They ain't a bad band either.'

'Trust Wally to be away when anything happens,' sighed Jethro. 'OK, I think I've got the feel of this thing now, all we can do is wait and see what happens – if anything does happen.'

It was almost ten minutes before anything did happen and that came in the form of a slow and seemingly deliberately heavy tread on the boardwalk outside the saloon. The sound was heard by the remaining customers and there were a few uneasy shuffles and very quiet whispers between them followed by apprehensive glances at the front door and quick glances at the back door. However, they chose to remain where they were.

It was probably no more than about thirty seconds; but seemed more like two or three minutes, before a very dirty, bent figure pushed its way through the swing doors and stood for a few moments blinking in the light before appearing to see Jethro. The figure straightened itself up as much as the ungainly growth on his back would allow, hooked the thumbs of both hands into the top of his belt and sneered at the lone figure by the counter.

'Thought I was dead didn't you?' he grated. 'Well,

maybe I am, maybe I am, in which case you won't be able to kill me twice.'

'I thought you'd drowned,' admitted Jethro.

'It'd take more'n a young whipper-snapper like you to drown me,' hissed Humpback. 'I found Pete an' Ernie, they was dead all right. I guess that just leaves me to kill you. You made the mistake of leavin' a horse an' saddle behind. Now, Mr Jethro Smith, I'm either goin' to kill you or you're goin' to kill me. I ain't got nothin' to lose, I was told about six months ago by a doctor from back East that I have somethin' he called cancer. Don't know what that is but it means I ain't got very long to live. He reckoned no more'n a year an' he's probably right, so I reckon I might as well take you out with me, either that or die in the attempt. I hear you're pretty damned good with that gun of yours, well, I got news for you, I've been pretty damned good a whole lot longer'n you have. Go on, son, you make the first move.'

Jethro would have been much happier had Humpy come into the room shooting, he would not have had a problem. As it was, his logic told him that he ought to shoot first, but he had a natural revulsion to killing in cold blood, especially remembering that he had killed Curly Johnson in cold blood and that he had even felt some satisfaction which had frightened him. Very slowly and quite deliberately he turned his back on the humpback, knowing full well that he was taking a great risk, but he had to force him into making the first move. This appeared to have the desired effect as Humpy suddenly screamed out at him.

'No man don't ever turn his back on me!' he yelled. 'OK, feller, if that's the way you want, it don't matter none to me. . . .' Jethro heard the rustle of clothing and the slight rasp of metal on leather as he turned. . . .

There were two shots, one of which seared across Jethro's upper arm but caused no real damage and the second which thudded into the chest of Humpback Chisholm. This time there was absolutely no doubting that Chisholm was dead, but at the same time there appeared to be a very satisfied smile on the old man's face.

'I really believe he wanted me to kill him,' said Jethro, glancing up at a ring of faces. 'He really wanted to die.'

'Maybe so,' agreed Jimmy, 'but he also meant to kill you, you just got lucky, that's all.'

'Then maybe I'd better leave while luck is still with me,' said Jethro.

Nobody actually heard his wagon leave, but it was found to be gone before dawn the next day.